Numbering All the Bones

Ann Rinaldi

SCHOLASTIC INC.

New York Toronto London Auckland Sydney
Mexico City New Delhi Hong Kong Buenos Aires

For Noni and Vern

ISBN 0-439-44948-0

12 11 10 9 8 7 6 5 4 3 2 1   2 3 4 5 6 7/0

Printed in the U.S.A.   40

First Scholastic printing, September 2002
The text for this book is set in 10/17 Baskerville BE Regular.

THEY HAVE PIERCED MY HANDS AND MY FEET.
THEY HAVE NUMBERED ALL MY BONES.

—DAVID THE PSALMIST

*Yesterday on the way home from the stationer's in Washington
City, I saw the ring in a pawnshop.*

*My brother Neddy's ring. Sitting there, pretty as you please,
on a piece of black velvet, all ready for some woman's hand. As
if it never had been buried in a grave. As if nobody was ever sold
away because of it.*

*I stood looking at it, wondering who would buy it, and would it
bring them any good fortune. And a whole trainload of thoughts
raced through my head, like the trains that used to come through
Andersonville three, four, five, even six times a day after the prison
was opened.*

*The train in my head dumped off thoughts like those trains
dumped off prisoners.*

*How, before the prison opened, the train only came through twice
a day. One up from Albany at eleven in the morning, the other
down from Macon at one-thirty in the afternoon. How we marked
the doings of the day by those whistles.*

*How Mr. Hampton would say, "God is in his heaven, all is
right with the world," when he heard the whistles.*

How, once they opened the prison, God wasn't anywhere

near Andersonville. God skedaddled, like a hare before one of Mr. Hampton's hounds.

How Miz Gertrude used that ring as an excuse to accomplish her own evil ends. How my brother Zeke found it for her when it was lost. How brother Neddy used it to keep me hoping. And I used it as an excuse to work at the cemetery.

Oh, my thoughts came tumbling off that train that was rushing through my mind like all those Yankee soldiers used to, dazed and benumbed and weary.

And I remembered then how I'd promised Miss Clara I'd write down what I recollected about the prison. Because she wants to write herself a book. Only I never could get it all straight.

How I came to be at the prison. At first I thought it was about the ring. Then I said, no, it was about the bones we buried. Or reburied there. And then yesterday, standing in front of the window of that pawnshop, looking at that ruby-red ring, I was finally able to admit that it was about me.

And that if I write about my time at the prison that summer, I have to go back to before. Because evil never springs up out of the Lord's good earth and happens on its own. Always it's from the seed of what's been planted before.

Of course, we all know what brought it into being, what came before.

Evil. There was an overabundance of it in Georgia at that time. It grew with the crops, the cotton and the corn and the grain. It grew lush, like the peaches. People ask now, "How can you people have lived all around that place and not known what went on there, inside the walls?"

Nobody believes that most people didn't, that people can go about their daily chores and lives and tolerate evil amongst them. But many did. I did, and the people on Pond Bluff did, and the onliest reason I got tangled up in the evil at the prison was because of that ring, sitting there on that black velvet in the pawnshop window.

Ain't that a thunderation?

Miss Clara says all that is necessary for evil to exist is for good men to do nothing.

I would add, women. I would add, me. And I would go back now and try to write about it for Miss Clara.

CHAPTER ONE

Some Plain Facts, and How Sancho and Moll Came Home

THE END OF FEBRUARY, YEAR OF OUR LORD Eighteen Hundred and Sixty-Four. That's as good a place as any to start, I suppose, though I may have to do some backtracking so things are set straight.

First, let me set some facts down plain. Miss Clara is a great one for setting facts down plain.

I was thirteen already. Lord A'mighty, as my mama used to say, who'd of thought it? I was too tall, the dresses Mistis handed me down from Annalee, the master's daughter, just about skirted my ankles, were always short in the sleeves, and loose in the bosom. Oh, how I wished I had more bosom, like Annalee, who was the same age and always made me feel so wanting. I was just getting to that part of my growth where I didn't know what to do with my long legs and ungainly hands when I was in the presence of a man. Just noticing how perfect and beautiful everybody else was, even Iris in the kitchen, who always tormented me. And always knew what to do with her hands and legs, especially around Homer, who worked in the fields.

I was a house slave, if you want to get legal about it. But there was nothing about my condition that was legal. I slept in the house, I was educated by Mistis and hardly had any chores. And there was always the promise in the air that I would be taken care of proper-like when Mr. Lincoln's "great measure" was put into action.

Mistis talked a lot about Mr. Lincoln's "great measure." She was the master's second wife. I was his daughter, but not by his first wife. It gets powerful mixed-up, here. My mama was the cook in the kitchen before Iris.

That's enough plain talk for now, except to say the crops were good that year at Pond Bluff. That's the plantation where I lived, just outside Andersonville, Georgia.

Our workers were few, though. Onliest ones left were Man-Jack and Boy-Jack, Octavius, and Toomy. And Toomy had only one hand. The Confederates took him to work at the munitions factory in Macon two years before, his hand got blown off, and they sent him back to us.

Roper and Homer were at the prison for the last month, helping to build more stockade fencing. The man who came 'round said he had the authority to take them.

"Seems like everybody's got authority anymore but me," Mr. Hampton said.

His true name is Mr. Hampton Kellogg. But I call him Mr. Hampton. "You people with authority gonna do me and my plantation more harm than the Yankees," he said.

Of course we still had Octavius, but his bones creaked. If so many of the hands hadn't already run off, Octavius would have been sunning himself down on the little hill by the pond.

Then there was Iris, who had taken over the kitchen since my mama died. Four female slaves had run off last year to join the Yankees over the border in their winter quarters in Kentucky. Patsy, Moll, Keesha, and Sary. Moll was wed to Sancho. I suppose I ought to say she "jumped the broom" with him. Lordy, my language is half slave and half white, just like me. Anyways, in any language, Sancho was a good worker and much missed.

The men who'd run, besides Sancho, were Quince and Ry-Bert. And my brother Neddy.

I'd known Neddy was going to run. He was sixteen already, tall and strong and handsome and always talking about the Promised Land in the North. It broke my heart the way he talked of it.

And he hated Mistis. "She's no better than his first wife, Miz Gertrude," he told me more than once. When I asked him how he could say such when Mistis was a Yankee and had taught him to read and write, he scoffed. "She doesn't do anything unless it's for her own good," he said. "Yankee? She's no Yankee. She's only down here to make money on the war. If she was for the Yankees why didn't she let me go join the army when I asked her? I have to run. And she'll never let you leave neither, sister of mine. You set your cap on freedom on your own. Don't wait 'til she gives permission, 'cause she's never gonna give it. And don't trust her, ever."

Neddy wrote to me once. The letter was given to me by Mr. Hampton, on the sly. The envelope was filthy and crumpled.

Neddy was with the Eighth United States Colored Troops in Kentucky. *Word is we'll be moving out soon, South,* he wrote. *I am doing well, except that we can't seem to get our hands on any salt. We heard there are warehouses in the South full of salt owned by people making money on the war. Don't I recollect Mistis Jennie and her brother trading in salt? Keep your ears open about such things.*

One of my friends here is from Ohio. His name is Thomas

Eston Hemings. Says he is the grandson of Thomas Jefferson.
Think on that.

I thought on a lot of things in the year Neddy left. Was he right about Mistis? I didn't know. As for her never giving me my freedom, the law would be the law once the Yankees came, wouldn't it? And we all knew by spring of '64 that they'd be coming. It was just a matter of time. Mr. Hampton said he knew it since Gettysburg, last summer.

Oh, I allow there are ways of holding on to people that don't have to do with any law. And it scared me, because I didn't know, when push came to shove, if I'd have the mettle to leave and go against Mistis.

So I'd push Neddy's words from me, and remind myself how, before Mistis came, my life was worse than a wild hog rooting around in the woods. I just kept reminding myself that, is all.

❧ · ❧

That morning in February was mild, and I went down hungry to breakfast. I was still taking some meals at the table with them, still fooling myself into thinking I was part of the family. Still taking Iris's dirty looks when she served.

"Sancho and Moll are back," Mr. Hampton told me as I sat down.

"Didn't he like the army?" I asked. I thought of Neddy. Could you leave the army if you didn't like it?

Then I thought, Sancho and Moll ran. Will Mr. Hampton punish them?

As if reading my thoughts, Mistis said it. Right out. "Well I hope you punish them good, Hampton." Then she looked at me and flushed. "Our people have been so burdened by their absence."

"What worries me," Mr. Hampton said, "is, what is Sancho now? A runaway from the United States Army? And if I shelter him, am I in trouble?"

"He belongs here," Mistis assured him. She was dark haired, slim, and right pretty. Mr. Hampton was smitten with her.

"Do they bring any news of Neddy?" I asked.

Mistis laughed. "Now, him I am really put out with, that brother of yours, Eulinda. After all I did for him." She said it playfully, but somehow I had reason to think she meant it.

"No word of Neddy, as far as I know." Mr. Hampton stood up. "Why don't you go down to the quarters and hear what you can hear and let us know, Eulinda?" he asked. "I'll be in my study. And tell Man-Jack and Boy-Jack I expect them to get started plowing that south field today."

I knew Iris was listening in the hall. And I knew she'd tell the others.

"Did you have that dog in your bed last night?" Mistis asked after Mr. Hampton left the table.

"Otis always sleeps with me."

"Well, if those bed linens smell, you'll wash them your-self. I'll not put Iris to the task."

"Otis doesn't smell," I reminded her.

"All dogs do, especially one that roams the barnyard. I swan, Eulinda, I do wish you wouldn't give in so to the darker side of your nature."

She tried to talk like a Southerner, and it always came out wrong. I blushed. "Yes, ma'am."

"That dog of yours needs a washing. I insist he be washed with lye soap, then lavender water. And you have lessons today. You don't keep a good writing hand with-out practice."

I walked on the fancy brick walkway into the detached kitchen. I did have a good writing hand. Mistis, and often Mr. Hampton, too, asked me to pen letters for them.

Iris was taking a loaf of bread from the oven.

"Can I take it to the quarters?" I asked.

She humphed. "You best take sumpin' if you expect to bring back gossip," she said.

"I don't bring back gossip, Iris." I did sometimes, to

my own shame. And I liked doing it less and less. All they talked about in the quarters these days was what they were going to do when the Yankees got here.

"You know I love everybody in the quarters. I wouldn't do that."

She wrapped the bread in a towel and handed it to me. "You doan know who you love," she said, "thas' your trouble."

I hugged the sweet-smelling, warm bread close to me as I went out the back door of the kitchen, down to the quarters, my little smelly dog, Otis, trailing behind.

≈ • ≈

I heard the laughter from Sancho and Moll's cabin, saw smoke coming out of the chimney where no smoke had come for near a year, and stepped quickly onto the porch.

First I listened. Not so's I could bring back gossip, but because they hushed like a flock of crows hearing gunshot when I joined them.

"I heered they be here by the end of the summer." It was Man-Jack's deep voice. I knew he spoke of the Yankees.

"Praise the Lord," Octavius said. Then: "You feel poorly 'bout leavin' the army?"

Sancho answered no.

"Doan they 'low womens and chil'ren?" Boy-Jack asked.

Sancho said yes. "They's whole colored families with the army in the west. Babies in arms. Babies 'bout to be birthed. Knee-high children."

"Then why you come home?" Boy-Jack asked, pushing.

"'Cause there weren't enough food for Moll, and we worry 'bout sickness. 'Cause I couldn't always be wif' her. Sherman be talkin' 'bout movin' out into Georgia in May. I couldn't leave Moll."

I stepped inside. They all looked up from where they were sitting around Moll's old wood-plank table and smiled. I set the bread down. "For your homecoming," I told Moll.

She didn't know I was lying. She got a knife and started to slice it. "This place is gonna need a whole day's cleanin'" she said.

I saw right off that she was expecting a child. Her dress, soiled and ragged from travel, stuck out in front over a round belly. I kissed her. "I'll help you," I said. "Glad you're home." I kissed Sancho, too.

"Lookit you," Moll held me away from her. "Growin' so, it's disgraceful! Your mama should see you now. And Neddy! Gettin' prettier every day, Eulinda girl."

Sancho looked up at me, grinning, and winked. "I heered 'bout Mr. Julian," he said. "Any word of him?"

Mr. Julian was Mr. Hampton's son, off fighting for the Confederacy and missing since Christmas.

"No," I said.

Iris came up on the porch and into the one-room cabin. "And Master, he's half here and half there and all the way inta nowhere since Julian disappeared," she said. She gave Sancho and Moll hugs. And I thought, Yes, that's just what Mr. Hampton's been of late. Only I'm too namby-pamby to say it.

And then I thought, I'm starting to think like a white person, covering everything up, lying to myself, and prettifying every dolorous thing.

I watched them all for a moment. I fetched myself a cup of coffee. And when there was a break in the conversation, I asked Sancho, "How is Neddy?"

"He left with the Eighth. Went afore Christmas," Sancho said.

I nodded. Then, of a sudden I felt uncomfortable in the silence that followed. I saw their eyes meet across the table, saying things I wasn't part of. And I knew they wanted to talk without me.

"I set your traps by the stream," Boy-Jack said finally. "They should be checked today, Eulinda."

I thanked him. "Did Neddy send any note for me before he left?" I asked Sancho.

"He didn't know I was comin' back," Sancho said. Then he laughed. "I didn't know it yet then, either."

More laughter. The air was so heavy with words that needed saying it was near exploding like the munitions works in Macon.

I finished my coffee and said thank you and that I'd be back in a bit. I was going to check my traps. It was a fine morning for it. I picked up a basket and a knife and called Otis and went out the door. All the while telling myself, Well, Eulinda, if they don't trust you, it's your own doing. What do you expect, girl? You can't have everything.

I was halfway to the barn when I heard footsteps behind me and Sancho calling softly. "Eulinda, hold on a bit."

I stopped and waited. Sancho had tight, curly hair and a ready smile, and he was built like a blacksmith. He and Moll were near thirty by now. Since Mama had died six years before, they were the nearest to a mammy and pappy I'd ever had.

"Gotta tell you somethin'. He took my elbow and guided me behind the corn crib. "You asked about Neddy."

My heart leaped. "Yes."

"He did send a message. You remember that ring?"

Not too many people knew of the ring. Sancho and Moll were the only ones on the place, besides Mr. Hampton, who even remembered when my brother

Zeke was accused of stealing it. "How could I forget?"

"He's still got it, Eulinda. He says he's gonna hold on to it, 'til after the war. Then sell it to stake you and him when you go west."

I smiled. Neddy had always wanted to go west. Tears came to my eyes. And so many thoughts crowded in front of me I could scarce see the fields and fences, the trees and ridges. "Thank you, Sancho," I said.

CHAPTER TWO

Remembering the Rabbit in the Celery Patch, and How I Saw My First Yankees

I CAN THINK ABOUT THAT RING ANYTIME, anywhere, and keep ironing a dress, singing in church, or cooking up a mess of collard greens while I'm thinking.

But I can't ever think on my little brother Zeke without I have to sit down all alone, off from everybody.

That morning he came to me, Zeke, the way he sometimes does, making me all quiet and giggly at first, then getting such a hold on my heart that I'm bawling like a stuck pig. Which is why I have to be alone, away from everybody.

I sat down in the tall grasses above the creek. And I heard his laugh so clear you'd think he was hiding in the grasses, like he sometimes used to do. Zeke gets my mind all jumbly.

You see? Now I have to get some facts down plain again.

I was Miz Gertrude's private girl. Remember she was Mr. Hampton's first wife? Well, she died, and the how of it I'll get to in a minute.

I was brought into the house to fluff her pillow, rub her feet, and fan the flies off her. Being the same age as her Annalee, I'd serve her, too. Annalee got all kinds of good food. I'd stand there hungry, waiting for her to finish so I could get the scraps. But before Miz Gertrude handed me the dish, she'd spit into what was left, so I couldn't eat it.

She was seven kinds of evil, that woman. I don't know why she wanted me in the house, but she never did these mean things in front of Mr. Hampton. Behind his back she'd do her mischief to me. Which included saying all kinds of bad things, so I didn't get any notions about being smart.

"Bright yellows are stupid," she'd say. I was called a "bright yellow" because of my light skin.

When company came she'd dress me in Annalee's castoffs.

Visitors would remark what a lovely child I was, and try to speak to me. Oh, Lordy, there was trouble! If they made too much of a fuss over me, I'd be punished after they left for being "pushy." She'd slap me. "Who do you think you are, Miss Bright Yellow?"

I'd scream, and she'd laugh.

Mr. Julian, who is lost somewhere now up in Yankee-land, was good to me. He'd sneak me vittles on the sly. But he was sent off to school. And Annalee went to the local girls' academy.

My father worked at another plantation ten miles away. I saw him only twice a year when he and Mama were allowed to visit.

Miz Gertrude liked to have me clean her chamber pot. She'd stand over me. "Put your hands right in there," she'd say. "Right in." Or she might decide I needed a purge and make me drink a foul-smelling liquid that gave me the dry heaves. Oh, she was Miss Devil-Boots all right, with her pretend-yellow hair that she rinsed with some mix that came from her sister in Macon. She had brown eyes with a strange light in them. And she held sway over Mr. Hampton. And she could make him cringe, hinting of the reason.

❧ · ❧

I found out the reason from my big-mouth brother Neddy, when I was seven. "Mr. Hampton's your daddy," Neddy told me.

"My daddy's at Pound Ridge," I said.

"Your daddy's right here," Neddy insisted. "Mine's at Pound Ridge."

I cried then, because I understood. On plantations

there's always whisperings about whose daddy is whose. Whisperings and lies.

"Then why doesn't he take up for me if he's my daddy?" I asked my brother.

"It just ain't done, masters taking up for any children from a slave woman." Shoved it right in my face, Neddy did.

When I was seven my mama had another baby—my little brother Zeke. He had bright, beautiful eyes and the roundest, most cunning face I ever did see. His mind was as quick as a rabbit's in the celery patch. And you know how you feel about a rabbit in the celery patch. It's always in the way, but you look for it if it's not there.

Zeke came up to the big house every day. I used to help Mama in the kitchen. When he came to the door, he'd smile so, all the hope of the world in his eyes as he thought of what fun he'd have that day. I loved Zeke so, and Miz Gertrude knew it.

Stupid I was to show it in front of her, to laugh and shriek with him and hug him close. There she was, just waiting all those years since I was born, for a way to get back at me and mama. Like a fox in the bushes.

One day she misplaced her ruby ring, the one handed down to her from her grandmother. It was worth a lot of money and she was beside herself.

Zeke found it on the fancy brick walk that went from

the house to the kitchen. I saw him pick it up and run to her with it.

Instead of saying thank you she scooped it up and screamed. "This child stole my ring!"

She was near hysterical. We couldn't quiet her or convince her otherwise. "That's what comes from letting the Nigras roam the house. Theft!" she said.

Mama begged her to see the truth. She wouldn't. And Mr. Hampton was away in Atlanta on a business trip. The next day she sent me and Mama and Neddy on an errand to town. And when we came home Zeke was gone.

Mama ran all around Pond Bluff looking, wringing her hands, praying. She swore he fell into the pond. Then Octavius got hold of her and told her what had happened.

Some white men had come in a wagon, he said. Slavers. And they took Zeke away. Mama fainted dead on the ground. I screamed and ran until I couldn't run anymore, then lay down on the red clay of the Georgia earth, the only bosom I had to cry on. Then I ran into the house and screamed at her. "If you're angry because Mr. Hampton is my daddy, why not sell me?"

She drew her hand back halfway to Maine, that woman, and slapped me. I lost all my senses.

They had to tie Neddy up that night in the quarters to keep him from running off to bring Zeke back. Mama stayed with him, telling him she needed him, not hanging from a tree or beaten to death, but here, with her and me.

When Mr. Hampton returned he was angry, but could do nothing.

No more quick little rabbit in the celery patch. I dream about him so often. Always, I'm opening the kitchen door and he's coming up the steps with that bright look in his eyes. And I'm holding out my arms. Then he's gone.

※ · ※

My mama killed Miz Gertrude for what she did. Not with a knife or a gun. Not even with poison. She used herself.

A little while after Zeke was sold, God brought His big fist down on Pond Bluff. Sickness came. Malignant fever. All the other servants came through all right, but not Mama. She got powerful sick. None of Mr. Hampton's remedies, not even his poultices of warm ashes and vinegar, helped. So he sent for Dr. Bedford Head, who said Mama had a touch of cholera, too, and should be kept away from everybody.

Then one day Mr. Hampton was in town playing billiards and Mama came into the house. I was there, helping Iris in the kitchen. And I stood like a jackass in the rain while Mama went right by us, into the main part of the house, into the parlor where Miz Gertrude was writing some letters.

Miz Gertrude like to jump out of her chair, seeing Mama standing there all feverish and talking to herself. I crept into the hall to watch. And there was Mama hugging Miz Gertrude and saying how sorry she was that she couldn't work in the kitchen anymore. There Miz Gertrude was, saying "Please, please, it's all right, go back to your cabin. Let me go."

But Mama wasn't about to let go. She hugged Miz Gertrude, she slobbered all over her, then she turned and went by me in the hall, back to the quarters, where, that night, she died.

Two days later Miz Gertrude came down with the cholera. In a week she was dead. And Mr. Hampton knew nothing about Mama coming into the house. And me and Iris never told him.

∾ . ∾

Mr. Hampton married Miss Jennie Ambrose of Lowell, Massachusetts, and Atlanta a year later. Her brother, Phineas Ambrose of Atlanta, a renowned businessman, gave her away.

I don't remember my first daddy much. But I recollect one thing he used to say to Mama when they visited. "You don't trade in the devil you know for the one you don't know," he used to say. And he was right.

∾ . ∾

After they built the prison a mile from Pond Bluff, game got scarcer than horns on a rabbit. The men working on the place must have killed or scared away all the deer, rabbits, and possum. If I had been a deer, I'd have skedaddled, too.

But I had three rabbits in the traps Boy-Jack had set. Otis was all fired up, showing me where to find them. I put them in my basket and was about to go back home when I heard the voices.

Nobody hears voices in these parts unless they're seeing haints or drinking too much corn liquor. I stood on a little hillock, looking down at the red clay road. I could smell the stink of the prison from here, worse than any outhouse. Then I saw the soldiers.

Yankees! Leastways they were dressed in blue. They didn't look like much though. All ragged-like and dragging themselves like yesterday's parade. I'd never seen a Yankee soldier before, lessen you counted Sancho. And he didn't count, because I knew him before he went for a soldier.

All the Yankees we'd heard about were sharp and smart in appearance. Well-fed and sassy. These were anything but. Then it came to me.

These were prisoners! And they were being herded along by some Confederate guards. Those were the voices I'd heard. Some of the Yankees were even shackled, the way Confederates had shackled Toomy when they came to take him off to work. Some of the guards hit the stragglers with their rifle butts.

I didn't think I was that near the prison. They must have added another part. I wondered if it was the part Roper and Homer were working on, and if I'd see them.

I crept down the slope. Nobody saw me, and I stood behind some weeds, staring. Up ahead of the ragged line of men was a stockade. Tall, raw timbers stuck out of the ground making a fence near twice as tall as a man. It looked like some giant's bleached bones. Above it were turrets, with guards on them. Men with guns, pacing.

It all mushroomed out of the Georgia land, like somebody's nightmare come to life. I'd seen Annalee's books of fairy tales, and it looked like the kind of castle a man would make if his crops failed. I stood watching as the shouting guards herded the men toward the gate, which opened like the mouth of a dragon.

One or two men fell in the road and the guards kicked them, cussed at them, and threatened to shoot. I was frightened and rooted to the spot all at the same time. Never had I seen white men treated so.

Then I turned to go finally, only to be confronted by a man in a Confederate uniform, pointing a gun at me.

"You got a pass, girl?" he said.

CHAPTER THREE

How the Yankees Almost Put Otis in a Stew, and Mr. Hampton Finally Decided to Act Like a Father

"WHAT?"

"You stupid darkie. You got a pass to be out heah on this road?"

Otis started to growl and bark. "Shut that dog up, or I'll kill him," he ordered.

I picked Otis up and shushed him. He was trembling all over.

"Where you from, girl? You a runaway?"

"No, sir." I patted Otis. "I've been roaming these woods and fields long as I can remember."

"Don't get mouthy, girl, or I'll haul you over to Captain Wirz at the prison. You wanna go to prison?" He raised the gun barrel directly at me, and I thought at first that he was somebody to be reckoned with. He wasn't a full-grown man, though. Just an overgrown boy. Looked more like the scarecrow my brother Neddy had once made for the melon patch. No older than Boy-Jack, who was coming on to fifteen. His face was thin, his eyes had not quite decided to be blue, and his hair didn't have the gumption to be red. He had no sap in him. White trash.

"I said, where you from? Who you belong to?"

"I live over at Pond Bluff. Mr. Kellogg is my master. And he's got some eminence hereabouts."

Then Otis contrived to attack. He leaped from my arms to the ground and started in growling and gnawing at the scarecrow's pants cuff. Otis would attack anything, even a painter cat. Fool dog had no more sense sometimes than a fire ant.

"Git your mangy dog offa me, girl! Or I'll kill him."

"Otis, come here!" I knelt and picked him up, but he wasn't about to be hushed. I didn't know what all to do. Then the scarecrow took a dirty old rag out of his pocket. "Wrap this around his mouth. Or I'll blow his brains out here and now."

I did so. Then he reached out and took Otis from me, tucked him under one arm and with the other kept the rifle pointed at me.

"You give me back my dog!"

He took a step backward. "Do you know what them soldiers inside that prison get to eat every day?"

I shook my head, no.

"A handful of cornmeal, a thimble of meat, and some fodder corn. This doggie would smell powerful good frying in one of those Yankee skillets. Any one of them Union men would pay some handsome Yankee greenbacks for him."

"You can't!" I objected. "You have no right!"

"Right? What's a little slave gal know about rights? You got no rights, girl. Didn't they teach you that? Yer mighty mouthy for a female wench. Talk awful pretty, it seems to me. Somebody been educatin' you over there at that Pond Bluff place?"

I'd said too much. "My mistress is quality," I told him. "I try to speak like she does."

He accepted that, thank heaven. "Git yerself a pass afore you roam around again. He started walking toward the gate. I lifted my skirts and ran up the slope and across the fields to home, scraping my legs on the briars and crying all the way.

❧ • ❧

I hoped Mr. Hampton was home and had his wits about him. He was no more than half here and half there since Mr. Julian was missing, as Iris had said. She didn't know the half of it. He'd taken to having "fits." That's what Mistis called them. Some days he'd go off somewhere in his head. Go into some kind of a trance, stay that way for about an hour, then when he came out of it, he'd look around and say, "What's going on?" And never realize that he'd been somewhere else for the last hour.

When I reached the edge of Pond Bluff, first person I saw was Octavius, coming from the springhouse with a large piece of raw meat in hand. "What you runnin' from, Eulinda?"

"I'm running to. Where's Mr. Hampton?"

"Walkin' on the piazza."

Oh, Lordy. The piazza went all around the house. Mr. Hampton had calculated that it was sixty feet around and if he walked it eighty-eight times, he would have walked a mile.

"You look a sight, Missy," Octavius said.

"A guard at the prison took my dog."

He scowled. "What you doin' at the prison?"

"He says he's gonna sell him to a prisoner to make stew. I've got to find Master. I'll see you later."

He wasn't in front of the house, so I ran around to the back, and near bumped into Moll, who was feeding the chickens in the yard. I dashed by her. "Mr. Hampton! Sir!"

I never called him Daddy. I knew he was and he knew he was, and that was as far as it went. As far as anybody around Pond Bluff would take it. It wasn't something you went spouting off about. It was like swamp water we had to swim through every day, both of us, to get to each other. Did you open your mouth while swimming through swamp water? No, what master called the "noxious miasmata" would kill you.

I fell into step beside him. "Mr. Hampton, sir, a guard at the prison took my dog and they're going to eat him."

"How many times have I told you not to bother me when I'm walking, Eulinda?"

"Sir, did you hear what I said? They're going to have Otis for supper!"

He stopped. "I told you not to go near that prison, didn't I?"

"I didn't know I was near it, sir. They've built a new part, right near the small stream where I was checking my traps."

He made a sound of contempt and recommenced walking. "They need a new part. Train lets off prisoners five, six times a day now. It is causing a putrescent effluvium in the air all around us."

"Yessir. But what are you going to do about Otis?"

"Do? Why should I do anything?"

"Because they're going to eat him for supper."

"Well, he'll be tough. Not good eating. They'll find that out soon enough, then. I've never eaten dog, but I have eaten possum, rabbit, and squirrel in my time. The meat is juicy, but I don't think dog meat has that consistency."

"Mr. Hampton, please! He's my dog!"

"Then you should have minded me."

"But why should Otis suffer? The guard just took him! Said I had no rights. And pointed his gun at me."

He stopped again. "A gun? At you?"

"Yessir, and I told him who you were, and how you were of eminence around here, but he didn't care."

"He didn't, hey?"

"No sir."

He stood looking over my head at some middle distance beyond me. He was a tall man, dressed in black trousers and frock coat, silk cravat even in midday. He sported a beard, but no mustache. His head was part bald, his eyes crinkled, his nose long and aristocratic. He was nothing if not dignified at all times.

"I have sworn I will never go near that place," he murmured, "because of Julian. How do I know that my son isn't in a Yankee prison somewhere?"

"Yessir." My heart sank.

"However, I can make an exception. Go now and

clean yourself up, Eulinda. You look a frightful sight. Mistis will not be happy. And you know we must keep Mistis happy."

"Yessir."

He stepped off the piazza and yelled for Octavius. "Bring around Tippo, get my gun, and fetch Sancho to come with me. If he wants to make up for running off he can be of help to me today."

As we stood and waited for Octavius to bring around Tippo, he looked down at me. "You shall have your dog back, Eulinda,"

For the first time in a long time, he sounded like a father. I watched him mount Tippo, grab his gun, yell for Sancho, and ride off. And I thought, for the first time in a long time, that he looked young and full of sand and like the Mr. Hampton I remembered.

＊ ・ ＊

But I was still a namby-pamby, able to be bought off by a new dress from Mistis, a kind word or look from master, or a place at the table with them when they dined alone. It was what Neddy had always despised in me, why there had been bad blood between us. He knew they not only owned me, they could buy me over and over again every day if I chose to let them.

＊ ・ ＊

I had my penmanship lessons in a fit of agony that afternoon, worrying about Otis. But I needn't have. Mr. Hampton and Sancho came home around four with Otis in tow. "Your dog has had a providential escape," he said to me. "Now he really needs a bath."

The master looked peaked, white around the edges, and there was something in his eyes that made me afeared of what he had seen in the prison.

I got a tub of hot water and some lye soap and scrubbed Otis good. He was small and shorthaired, and he loved a bath. Afterward I rinsed him with lavender water, and he smelled right pretty when I got finished; and I took him into the kitchen where Iris was making welcome-home supper for Sancho and Moll, along with cooking regular dinner.

"I'm going to eat with the other servants tonight," I told Iris. And I started to set the table. Then Mistis came in to check on things.

"Eulinda, we expect you at the table with us tonight," she said sweetly.

My face fell. "I was hoping to have some celebration supper right here," I said.

Right off she got her back up. "Didn't Mr. Hampton spend the afternoon getting your dog back?"

"Yes, ma'am."

"At considerable cost to himself, I might add. So you could honor us with your presence. For myself, I don't care. You can eat all the collard greens and hog jawbone you want with the other servants. But you know how lonely he gets since Julian is away at war and Annalee at school in Atlanta. You must decide if you wish to belong to this family or not, Eulinda."

And with that she left the room.

Iris gave me a look that said more than five pages from the Bible. "You'd best eat with them," she said.

So I did. But Mr. Hampton was poorly at supper. His neck hurt him, he said. His neck always hurt when he had what he called "a confrontation." But he wouldn't speak of the prison. So I was just as glad when Mistis sent me to the kitchen for one of Iris's remedies.

Leavings of the meal were scattered on the table when I got there, and Sancho was telling about the prison. "I feel bad seeing those men in that hellhole. They are the men I served with."

"You never did," Boy-Jack said.

Sancho gave him a patient look. "They from the same army," he said. "The army that's fightin' to free us. And they doan' even have proper tents against the heat and cold. Thousands of 'em are crowded into that pen. They say hundreds be dyin' every day, from no food and sickness."

Candlelight did not soften the looks on the others' faces.

"Never," Sancho said, "have I seen white men brought so low. It's bad. White people around here shouldn't let it happen."

"What do they care 'bout Yankees?" Iris asked. "Like you say, they's fightin' to free us."

"If they be Christian, they should care about human beings so treated," Sancho insisted. "God's gonna bring his wrath down on people who treat other humans so."

Sancho wasn't much on God. So when he invoked His name, everybody listened. They saw me then, and nodded. I gave Iris Mistis's request, and she prepared the remedy, putting it in a cheesecloth. I left, feeling I'd missed something important, and wished I'd been there with them at supper.

CHAPTER FOUR

How Captain Wirz Came, and I Find Out About Neddy

TWO WEEKS LATER CAPTAIN WIRZ HIMSELF came to the house. It was a warm day in March. I was helping Iris in the kitchen. We were working with white-oak bark and bloodroot, ginger and capsicum, brandy and calomel, to make some remedies.

Iris was good at finding herbs and making remedies. Mr. Hampton depended on her, and now she was teaching me.

When we saw this ridiculous-looking man dismount his horse on the front walk, we thought he was a peddler. He was an undersized toad of a man, first off. And he was wearing a calico shirt, belted over his gray trousers; a cravat; a small gray cap on his head; and two large revolvers in his belt.

I'd just taken a pot of Iris's mixture outside to cool, and he saw me and came on the walkway to the kitchen.

"You gott some vater, maybe, Missy?"

Iris gave him some. He sipped it. "Vere is your master, hey? Tell him Captain Wirz is here."

Iris sent me for Mistis, who came flying down the walk.

"You gott a nice place here," he told her.

"We like it," Mistis said. "May I know, sir, the nature of your visit?"

"I am from Camp Sumter."

"Andersonville," Mistis corrected him.

"Ve prefer Camp Sumter. Ya. Vat your servant making here, Missus? So many pots."

"Remedies," she said.

"Ya. I cud use some myself. Dis arm, dem damn Yankees hit me with minne balls near two years ago now. At Seven Pines. Dis arm no goot to me no more. Just cause pain."

His right arm hung useless at his side.

"You gott any medicine for de pain?" he asked.

"No, I'm sorry. I just have for diarrhea, gangrene, and fever."

I knew she was lying. I knew, too, that if he offered to pay her, she would sell to him. Mistis always had an eye out for making money. But he did not offer.

"So. Vell. Makes no difference. Vat I come for is to ask for servants to dig more trenches. I see you gott slaves in de fields."

"We've already given two servants," Mistis said. "We can't spare any more, or we won't have a crop this year."

"Dem damn Yankees," he said again. "Ve hear dey are schleppin' 'round and comin' to Georgia. By Gott, you don't vatch dem, they kill you, sure 'nuf. I got mine troubles keepin' order at de prison."

Then his beady eyes lighted on me. And I was reminded of a rodent. "Dat's a likely colored girl you gott there, sure 'nuf. My wife and daughters live in town. De need some help in de house. You cud maybe hire her out to me? I pay you."

Did Mistis hesitate for even a bit? I saw her look at me, and quickened with terror. Then she said no.

"I haf' de authority to take her, you know."

"I doubt it, Captain Wirz. The rule is, one of every four servants can be impressed by your prison. We've already given two."

He was still eyeing me. Then he saw Otis, asleep by the hearth. "Is dis de girl my soldier haf the fight vit de odder day?"

"Yes," Mistis answered, "and we don't appreciate the

way he threatened her. I thought my husband had settled the matter, anyway."

"My guard tolt me how vell she speak. Big words she uses. You teachin' her, maybe?"

"She has been with us since she was a baby, Captain. I consider myself well-spoken and educated. I speak well in front of my servants."

But he spoke to me. "I suppose you tink because dat fool Lincoln made out a piece of paper vit some words on it you soon be free. Is dat it? Vell, missy, is dat vy you so snoody?"

"No, sir."

"Vy don't you run off if you tink you free?"

"Some of our servants have, Captain," Mistis told him. "Which is why we so badly need the ones we have. This girl's brother ran off, but she won't, I guarantee it."

"Your brudder go wit de odder Niggers to the damn Yankee army, maybe, hey?" he asked.

I looked at my feet.

"I gott at my prison de colored soldiers, ya. Tink dey somethin', too. Ve capture dem at a battle in Florida. Ve gott vun, you shud see. He gott in his skull a bullet. All night he valks an' moans. Serve him right, damn Yankee."

"Please, we don't wish to hear any more about your

prison," Mistis said. "If it's all the same to you. And since my husband isn't here right now, I would ask you to go and not upset my servants."

He bowed and turned to go. Then at the door of the kitchen he took one more look at me. "Vat name your brudder use?" he asked.

"Sir?"

"Don't play stupid. You coloreds not dumb. I tink maybe I haf' him in mine prison. I tink maybe he is the one with the bullet in his skull."

"Sir, I must ask you to leave!" Mistis insisted.

"De people come, just to see my prisoners. Vat kind of people you gott 'round here that dey come vit picnic baskets and make a holiday of it?" he asked Mistis. "Dey come to stand on the parapets and see Yankees. And colored troops. Vat kind of people you gott 'round here?" he said again as he went out the door.

I burst into tears and ran out the back door. Mistis called after me and Otis came at my heels, barking, but I just ran and ran. Neddy! At the prison? With a bullet in his skull? I knew in my heart then that he was there. Maybe not the one with the bullet in his skull, but there. Hadn't Sancho said he'd gone south with the army? What else was south of us but Florida?"

⊰ • ⊱

I stayed out in the woods all afternoon. I missed my lessons. I wandered, half crazy. Neddy at the prison! A mile from us! I wondered if he still had the ring. Then found myself caring more about him than the old ring.

Neddy had crept into the house right after Miz Gertrude died and taken that ring, the one Zeke was supposed to have stolen. Not because he wanted to steal, not because he wanted the ring. But because "It's all we got for Zeke," he'd told me.

A ring for Zeke was wrong. He knew it and I knew it.

But not to take it would have been wrong too, he reasoned.

Only when I heard the sound of a horse and carriage on the road approaching the house, only when the sun was disappearing behind the peach orchid and I heard Sancho calling the others in from the fields, only when I saw the smoke rising from the cabin chimneys, did I venture up the hill behind the house.

Candles were lighted. I could see Mistis and Mr. Hampton at the dining-room table, Iris moving around them, serving. I was about starved. I went onto the piazza and stood outside the dining-room windows.

"I've half a mind to send her to work for Captain Wirz's wife for a while," Mistis was saying, "just to teach her what she has here."

"I want nothing to do with that man," Mr. Hampton replied. "Especially now, hearing about Julian."

What had he heard about Julian?

"I take it that means no," Mistis said.

"It does."

"The time is coming, Hampton, when you are going to have to leave the servants in my care. I think that man was here for more than soliciting servants this morning."

"What other reason could there be?"

"The letter you brought home from town to me, from my brother in Atlanta? We are suspected of Unionist activities."

"What activities?"

"Does it matter? You know that Phineas and I have many. If they prove it, they will come and destroy this place."

Phineas was her brother in Atlanta. We went to Atlanta three or four times a year. I loved it there and hated it, too. I loved the house, the busyness, the shops. I hated it because Mistis treated me like a servant there. She said she had to. People came and went in her brother's house. People were watching them.

You didn't sit a bright-yellow servant girl at your table in Atlanta unless you wanted to be accused of being a Secret Yankee. You made her sleep in the lean-to, polish

Miss Annalee's boots when that young lady visited from the Female Academy. You even slapped your bright-yellow servant girl on occasion, and made sure people saw it. Especially in the street, she explained. And you slapped her good.

On our last visit, that spring, she and Uncle Phineas had seemed to be talking in code. Everything had to do with salt. "Time to put salt in the wounds," he'd say. Or, "That man is the salt of the earth."

And I recollected Neddy's letter, and knew they were storing up salt in warehouses, waiting for prices to rise.

Is that what one did when one was a Secret Yankee? Wouldn't it be better to give the salt to the soldiers who needed it?

But I knew the answers. Mistis was playing it two ways. Pretending to be a Secret Yankee and making money on the war. And if the Confederate authorities found out, they'd confiscate everything Mr. Hampton had, and burn everything else.

"I must find something," Mistis was saying now, "to put me in good with the Confederates. Some good act to do. Yet something that doesn't offend our Yankee friends."

I sank down on the wooden floor of the piazza, befuddled by all I'd learned that day, and waited for them to finish.

"Mr. Hampton, sir, could you write me a pass?"

He was in his study. "Is that you, Eulinda?"

"Yessir."

He was at his desk measuring something. He was always either measuring or counting or thinking. He liked best what he called "angles and points of the compass and abstract thought." I had no idea what he was talking about. But sometimes he made me part of his experiments.

"You may as well come in and pay the piper, girl. You've been bad today, I hear. Mistis is angry."

I ventured into the study. "Yessir."

"You can't just run off for a whole afternoon and not do your chores or studying. You're too big for that now. Everyone around here has to pull his weight, especially with so many of my people gone."

"Yessir."

He said something strange then. "You know, Eulinda, I can't always protect you as I'd like to. The day will come when I won't be able to protect you at all. I feel I must tell you that."

Was I supposed to know what he meant? But I did. He meant, against Mistis. "Yessir," I said again.

"Now what is it you wanted?"

"A pass, sir. So I could go about and not get into trouble. They say there are sentries out on all the roads."

"There are. And what need have you to go on the roads, then?"

"I want to go to the prison. They say they allow visitors. I want to see."

"See what, Eulinda?"

But I did not answer. So he knew. "Ah, it's what Captain Wirz said today, isn't it? About your brother. Well, that man is a peevish, bitter little person with the brain of a gnat. Don't pay mind to him."

"Sir, Sancho said Neddy went south with his regiment. And Captain Wirz said he has colored prisoners captured in Florida."

He sipped a glass of sherry. "I have to give one-tenth of my crops this year to the Confederate government. That was the talk at the billiard hall today. I'd rather convert my corn to whiskey than sell or give any of it to the government. And plant cotton to send north than plant corn in the first place."

"Please, Mr. Hampton, can't I just make one trip to the prison? Suppose Neddy is there?"

He paid mind to me then. "How do you think I would feel if I thought some Northern women were peering at my son up in Elmira Prison? And gloating."

"Mr. Julian's in Elmira Prison?"

"I got some mail by a special rider today. Yes, he is."

"Sir, I'm not going to peer. Or gloat. I just want to see if Neddy's there."

"And if he is?"

I stared at him. I hadn't thought that far.

"Then I must bring him back, Eulinda. And there is no Confederate authority in Georgia who would deny the fact that Neddy is my property. But will he wish to come back? There is the question."

"Sir, from what Sancho said about that place, why wouldn't he?"

He sighed. "I think you do not yet know your own brother, Eulinda. Very well, I shall write you a pass. But if you go, you set certain actions in motion. You see this clock?"

He pointed to a little clock on his desk. He had had it made in Atlanta. It was of his own design. It was under glass, with a little wheel that spun and spun as the hours and minutes ticked away.

"I set that clock in motion," he said. "But if I interfere with that motion now, the clock will be broken. That is the responsibility we must take when we interfere with people's lives, Eulinda. That they may be broken."

"Yessir," I said again. But I knew I could never set anything into motion. Or stop anything or anybody from doing anything. I was helpless to do anything important. Why, when I made taffy it didn't even come out right. Mistis scolded me for wasting the ingredients.

But I agreed with him, and I waited while he wrote the pass. Like I already said, I didn't understand him half the time, but I knew I could always bring him around. He was about the only one in my life whom I could set in motion.

CHAPTER FIVE

How I Went to the Prison and Did Mistis a Favor Without Wanting To

I TOOK MOLL WITH ME TO THE PRISON NEXT day. Mr. Hampton had cautioned me not to go alone. She toted a sack.

"What have you got there?" I asked.

"Some sticks of wood, twists of tobacco, and a cow horn full of soft soap."

"What for?"

"To sell. Sancho said if I stand in the right place, I kin sell it to the soldiers they let out to bury the dead."

I shuddered. "I want nothing to do with it, Moll."

"You never do want to do with anythin'."

"If I knew you were going to start on me, I wouldn't have brought you along."

"I'm jus' sayin' you never wants to do with anythin'. Thas' because you doan' need anythin'. Got all your wants takin' care of. No need to git down on me fer tryin' to make some money."

"I'm not getting down on you. And who says all my needs are taken care of?"

She made a scoffing sound. "Anythin' you want, Mr. Hampton see that you git. You his daughter."

"I don't know, Moll," I said glumly. "I don't know how much it counts, being his daughter. I think Mistis isn't gonna let it count that much when push comes to shove."

"You finally figured that out?" She laughed. "That man ain't got a thought in his head anymore that she doan' put there. I'll tell you what though, if'n you listen."

"What?" I asked.

"You best git anythin' you gonna git from him while the gittin's still good."

"Now what does that mean?"

"Means while he's still in that head of his you better git somethin' from him. Afore Mistis gits it all. Means if'n he gits bad news about Mr. Julian, he gonna go all the way crazy and we all gonna be left in her hands. Tha's what it means."

"Are you worried about that, Moll? You and the others?"

"Why should we'uns worry? We'uns all be gone by then. War'll be over."

"So what makes you think I won't be gone, too?"

More laughter. "Child, you ain't never gonna leave here. You ain't got the mettle to leave, thas' why I know you won't be gone."

"Well," I said angrily. "Everybody better not be so sure."

She gave me a suspicious look. "You thinkin' 'bout leavin' when the time come, girl?"

"Why wouldn't I?"

She did not answer. But she reached out and took my hand as we made our way across the fields. "Time you thought 'bout it," she said. "You gotta make yourself come true, Eulinda. And if I'm still here, I'll help you. Any way I can."

Make myself come true. I liked the ring of it. I suppose it was the same as Mr. Hampton's clock, and setting things in motion. But I liked the way Negro people said it better.

Make myself come true. Yes, it had a ring to it.

❧ • ❧

We smelled the prison before we saw it. At the gates we went our separate ways. The last I saw of Moll, she was running off in the rutted muddy road, after some soldiers who had just come out with carts loaded with dead.

I turned to the entrance I'd first seen the day they took Otis. Three carriages were outside the gates with white folk in them. They were quality, here for a lark. The woman wore spring frills, toted parasols. The men were in good broadcloth. They escorted their ladies to the guards. There were at least six Southern ladies, all giggling with excitement as the men slipped the guards some coins to let them ascend the one parapet at this part of the prison.

"Kin fit eight up there." The guard turned to me. "You goin', girl?"

Immediately I saw that he thought I belonged to one of the white ladies, so I said yes. He handed us all crusts of bread.

"Are the colored troops near here?" I asked.

"Cain't tell who all is near where," he said. "The coloreds got their own place, but those no-count Yankees got no qualms 'bout mixin' the races."

I waited while the white ladies ascended, led by a guard. They held their ruffled skirts up with one hand. I followed discreetly behind. At the top there was more of a breeze. And more of a smell. The white ladies took out lacy handkerchiefs soaked in lavender and held them up to their noses.

The guard began to speak. "General Sidney Winder

was in charge of startin' this prison in January of this year. He's skedaddled back to Richmond. Left Captain Henry Wirz in charge. The prison ain't as big as needed. They gonna make it bigger. It's about two-thirds done. By the end of February we already had two thousand prisoners. By now we figure the count must be near ten thousand."

"No tents or barracks?" one lady asked.

"Ain't got any, Miss. What you see are shanties the men made from anythin' they kin get their hands on. They call them *shebangs*. You are now lookin' down on the south hillside, between the swamp and the stockade."

"What do they eat?" another lady asked.

"Last month they got a quart of tolerable-good meal, a sweet potato, and a piece of meat the size of a finger every day. This month the potato is gone, but they're given a quart of cow-peas for two hundred men a day. If'n they got any Yankee greenbacks, they kin buy from Confederate suttlers. Or local farmers. I've seem 'em eat anythin', even dog."

Two white ladies made gagging noises. I shivered, thinking how close Otis had come to being eaten.

Then I looked over the shoulder of one white lady, into the vast muddy enclosure. Never had I seen the likes of it! And I don't know what got filled up first—my eyes, my nose or my heart. On our plantation, animals were treated better.

What seemed like thousands of creatures were penned into acres of muddy ground. Ragged figures that were supposed to be men huddled in little groups about their shebangs. Small fires burned. The men were in tattered clothing, and packed so close you could scarce separate where one began and the other left off.

There was a hum in the air, too, which you didn't pick up on at first, but when your ears got a purchase on it, it seemed like it'd never go away. It was the men talking, but it had in it a note of low rage and helplessness.

I'd seen people packed together in the marketplace in Atlanta. But not like this. There was no color here. Everything was washed out in tones that had no hope, mud-gray and black. The men all seemed to have long hair, too. And beards. They were mournfully thin, and they did not walk, they ambled.

So many were on makeshift crutches. So many had haphazard bandages around their heads. Many dragged about on one leg. So many had missing arms.

I saw sticks in the ground with more rags attached. Then I minded that they were flags. One said 20TH INDIANA. Another said 9TH MARYLAND INFANTRY. There was something sad and desolate about those flags, stuck in the middle of the refuse. I looked for the colored troops, but I couldn't make out any dark faces. So many of the white men were dark from the sun.

Two white women were tossing bread over the parapet, calling out to the prisoners. The bread landed in a small area right below us that was sealed off by a wooden fence. I saw the prisoners look longingly at the bread, but make no move toward it.

"Why don't they get it?" a lady asked.

"Because it's inside the Dead Line. They go in there and they'll be shot dead," the guard told her.

"Throw it further," I said. "Here, give it to me, I'll throw it."

She turned to me, her smile fading, shocked that I would dare speak to her. Then she grabbed my arm and thrust me forward to the railing. "You Yankees down there," she yelled. "See this Nig gal up heah? Well, she's sister to y'all. Why y'all fightin'. Say hello."

I tried to pull back, but she wouldn't let me move. "Well, say hello!" she yelled again.

Nobody said anything. The woman laughed and released me. I pulled away, mortified.

Then the same white lady said something that distracted me from my shame. "I heard tell y'all got women prisoners heah."

"Three," the guard said. "Two were with their husbands in battle. They wear the uniform of the Union soldier. T'other was with hers on a wedding trip when their boat was taken by one of our revenue cutters off the coast of North C'alina. Some say she just give birth."

"Here?" Another lady dabbed her handkerchief over her face.

"Sure 'nuf," the guard said. "You wanna take in a boarder? Captain Wirz is lookin' fer a local family to take her an' the baby in. She's a mortification to him. Cain't have a baby here."

The ladies waved him off and we started down the steps. The show was over. On the ground the guard grinned at us.

"We also got the grandson of Thomas Jefferson. At least that's what the Nigger calls hisself. Says his name is Thomas Eston Hemings. Can you beat that, ladies? A Nigger in a Yankee uniform who says he's grandson of Thomas Jefferson. We got it all. Somethin' fer everybody. Send yer friends."

The muddy ground moved under me when he said that. Neddy had written to me about the grandson of Jefferson! They were friends! In the same regiment!"

Neddy was here!

Somehow I had to get Mr. Hampton to find him, to fetch

him home! Neddy couldn't stay here! I looked about for Moll, and saw her in the distance by the gate, waiting for me.

✵ · ✵

When we got back I could see from a distance that Mr. Hampton was walking the piazza again. Moll finished counting her Yankee greenbacks and shoved them into her sack.

"Doan' you tell anybody 'bout these," she said.

"I won't." I ran for the house where I fell in stride with Mr. Hampton. "What count are you up to?" I asked.

"I'm on my sixty-fifth turn, Eulinda. Are you all right?"

"Yessir. I'm just back from the prison."

"Are you happy with what you saw?"

"No. Lots of white ladies were there. When I left, the guard said they were killing off more Yankees at that place than twenty regiments of Lee's army."

"The four horsemen of the Apocalypse will soon be stalking the land around here, Eulinda, if they keep bringing more men into that place to die. Starvation, disease, pestilence, and death. And we will all suffer, the civilians in the whole countryside around."

I saw my opening. "Mr. Hampton, I know Neddy's there."

"Did you see him?"

"No sir. But the guard said they had the grandson of

Thomas Jefferson there. A Negro. And Neddy when Neddy wrote to me, he said he was friends with this man."

He kept walking.

"Mr. Hampton, we've got to get Neddy home. Please."

"Do you remember what I told you when you asked me for the pass? About seeking out Neddy?"

"Yessir."

"And not knowing him?"

"Sir, anybody would want to get out of there."

"Your brother left us, Eulinda. To go and fight with the army. That meant he chose possible death over being in bondage."

"But not imprisonment. He didn't choose that, sir."

He stopped walking. "Very well, I will go and fetch Neddy. But then you must be prepared for him to refuse to come home. Do you understand?"

I said I did. He recommenced walking. "Mr. Hampton, they've got women in there."

He closed his eyes. "Women?"

"Yessir. The guard said three. One just had a baby. And he said Captain Wirz is looking for a local family to board her and the baby."

"Are you asking me to take in a woman and a baby?"

"I don't know, Mr. Hampton. But don't you think it's a terrible place for them to be?"

"I certainly do." Mistis came up behind us, startling us both. "Hampton, listen to what the child is saying! It's the perfect situation I've been looking for."

"I wasn't aware you were looking for a situation, dear." He looked down at me as if to say, *I hope you're happy now, look what you've started.*

"Why, of course!" She rushed over to him. "Bringing that woman home would show my cooperation with the Confederate authorities and keep the Yankees happy. You did say she's a Yankee, didn't you, Eulinda?"

"Yes, ma'am."

"And Neddy!" She clasped me to her. "We'll bring him home, too. I'll send word 'round to the neighbors this afternoon. A call for baby clothes. And other supplies. I'll write a note to Dr. Head. He ought to examine the baby. Go find Sancho and Moll. Tell them I'll need them tomorrow for errands. And do come with us tomorrow to the prison."

And so it was done. Not the way I'd planned, but I suppose I shouldn't be fussy. She was on my side about bringing Neddy home. And I couldn't expect any more than that, could I?

CHAPTER SIX

How We Rescued a Woman and a Baby, and Mr. Hampton Was Right All Along

THE NEXT AFTERNOON MISTIS HAD BOY-JACK harness up the buggy and we went again to the prison. She'd sent a note to Captain Wirz, offering to take the woman with the baby, and he'd written back that he agreed.

The woman's name was Mrs. Hunt, he wrote. She would be able to leave this afternoon.

The buggy was piled with bundles, clothing, food, and medicines to give to Dr. Head, who was to meet us there, for use at the prison.

Mistis could be generous when the spirit seized her.

With us we took Moll and Sancho. Mr. Hampton came, too, riding Tippo. The prison ripped his heart out, he said, but he could not allow his wife to do this alone.

When we got there, he went directly to Captain Wirz's headquarters. Mistis went to the provost marshal's for a permit to carry goods through the line of sentinels. Dr. Head took the medicines right inside.

Moll, Sancho, and I waited in the buggy. Above us on the parapets, guards pointed guns at us. I counted seventeen cannon on the stockade walls. When Moll started to get down from the buggy with her sack, a crude-looking man holding two bloodhounds on a leash came over to us.

"Git back in, gal. No Nigras allowed to loiter 'round heah. You people cause more trouble than the damn Yankees. What you got in the sack?"

Moll got back in. At first she refused to answer, but Sancho nudged her.

"Ho-hound candy," she said. "Man who bought my tobacco twists last time said they'd kill fer ho-hound candy."

The dogs snarled and a guard came forward. "Trouble, Mr. Harris?"

The man he called Mr. Harris held out his hand for the sack. Moll recoiled. "This gal's a troublemaker," Mr. Harris said. "Won't hand over the sack."

"You all know who this is?" the guard asked. "Mr. Benjamin Harris. Owns nine of these dogs. Tear y'all to bits soon as look at you. He scours the countryside for escaped prisoners. But these hounds know no difference from prisoners and contentious people. You gonna hand over the sack or not?"

Sancho nudged Moll again. She handed over the sack. Mr. Harris plunged his hand in, took out the candy, thrust it into his pockets and gave the sack back. Then he let his dogs pull him around the outside of the stockade as they went about their business of sniffing.

"Bad." Sancho shook his head. "Those dogs'll kill people. Not right."

Mistis and Mr. Hampton came back within minutes of each other. "I'm not allowed to bring supplies in," Mistis said. "But we can go and find Mrs. Hunt. Are you coming, Hampton?"

"No. I've gotten permission from Wirz to visit the colored troops and maybe find Neddy. Sancho, you come along with me. Moll, you and Eulinda go with Mistis."

I watched Sancho and Mr. Hampton talking to one of the guards, then disappear inside the large gate, into the stockade, wishing I could go with them.

❦ · ❦

Her name was Janie. At least that's what she wanted us to call her. Not Mrs. Hunt. "I scarce had time to hear anyone call me that since I wed," she said.

She seemed to be so young. About seventeen. And in no

time at all she thought Mistis was sent by God. I guess I would too, if I lived in a tent that had its back ripped off, with my only possessions being a cot and a basket for the baby.

"I had a trunk with things from home," she told us, "but it is stolen. Some prisoners here do nothing but rob their fellow sufferers. All my clothing was in the trunk."

She wore a tattered dress. When she washed it, she said, she had to stay in the tent all day, wearing only her chemise.

Dr. Head examined the baby, a girl. Janie smiled at Moll and asked when her baby was due, like they were next-door neighbors, and she was not the rich daughter of a Massachusetts merchant and Moll a slave.

Moll told her. "Early summer."

Then Janie looked at me. "And who are you? Part of this group of angels?"

We took her and the baby home that very day. Dr. Head pronounced the child in good health. Mistis had brought some baby clothes.

On the way home I sat in the carriage with Janie, Mistis and the baby. Moll and Sancho were in the driver's seat. Mr. Hampton rode beside us. Mistis chatted all the way home, telling Janie about Annalee's room and how lovely it was and how it would be so good to see it occupied again.

At one point, my mind wandered. I was watching Mr. Hampton. His face was so grim that I knew he'd seen

Neddy. But he hadn't had the chance to speak of him yet.

Then I heard Janie gasp. "You own slaves?" she asked Mistis.

And I heard the lie from Mistis's own lips. "We care for them, my husband and I. We consider ourselves their guardians until such time as Mr. Lincoln's great measure comes into being."

"But he already signed the Emancipation Proclamation," Janie told her.

"Yes, but you can't free Negroes around here. Not now. Why we'd be ostracized by all our neighbors! Besides," said Mistis, lowering her voice, "They don't know my political leanings. I'm a Secret Yankee, you see."

Janie said yes. But I don't think she did see. Not any better than I ever had. Not at all.

❧ · ❧

"What is it?" I asked Mr. Hampton. "What has happened?"

He had summoned me to his study. Supper was late. Iris was bustling about in the kitchen, and Mistis was still getting Janie settled up in Annalee's room.

"Neddy would not acknowledge me."

"What? You saw him? He's there?"

He stood at the window in his study, looking out, his hands clasped behind his back. "I sent Sancho ahead to approach the colored troops while I spoke with the guard in charge. By the time I got there, Sancho had gained their trust. I recognized Neddy immediately. But he denied who he was."

My head was not taking this all in yet. "He denied it?"

"He said he was not Neddy Kellogg. He gave another name."

"What name?" I was aware that I was just echoing everything he said, sounding like an idiot, but what else could I do?

"I don't recollect. You'll have to ask Sancho. I only know he told the guard that he was a freedman. Not Neddy Kellogg, that he did not know me and would not come home with me."

"What did you do?"

"What could I do? His fellow prisoners backed him up. Said he was a freed Negro. So I left him there."

"But it doesn't make any sense," I said.

He turned to attend to papers on his desk. "I told you, didn't I, Eulinda? I told you about your brother. He left once. He won't come back again."

"But it's terrible there," I said.

"Yes," Mr. Hampton said. "It is terrible there. And I am shaken, to think he regards us as so bad that he won't have commerce with us anymore. I was always good to

Neddy, wasn't I?" His voice broke.

"It isn't you, Mr. Hampton," I started to say. I did say it, then broke off. Because he was seated at his desk now, his head in his hands. His hands were covering his face.

He was crying.

"Go, child, go," he said. "I have much thinking to do."

I went.

～⊛ · ⊛～

Moll was cooking. Sancho whittling on the porch, his chair tipped back, his feet on the palings. "Thought you'd be by," he said.

I sat down on the porch steps. "Tell me about Neddy. Was it truly him?"

"No other," he said.

"Did he know you?"

"Fer sure, though he didn't admit it."

"And how is he?"

"He's doin' just fine, Eulinda."

"Tell me, Sancho."

He sighed. "He's doin' just fine as can be expected in a place like that."

"And he refused to come home."

"Said he'd rather die a free Yankee soldier than come home an' be a slave."

Hopelessness gripped me. "Why, Sancho?" I asked.

He went about whittling for a bit before he answered. So I pushed. "Did he say anything to you? Did he ask after me?"

"Said nuthin' better than freedom," Sancho replied. "Said to tell you this."

So I knew then what Sancho wasn't telling me. Not in so many words anyway.

"He's doing it to show me. Is that it, Sancho? Is it to show me?"

"He never said such."

"You know Neddy. You've known him since he was a boy. You know how contentious he can be, and how we always argued about Mistis. I know she isn't what she says, Sancho. But what can I do? I can't run away and join the army, can I?"

He just shook his head, no.

"Is that all he said? Nothing else?"

"Said when the war is over, if'n he doan' get in touch with you, you're to go in there and find his bones."

"His bones?"

"Tha's what he say."

"But why? You mean he wants me to bury him back here? What does he mean?"

More whittling. "Think on it, Eulinda. Means he wants you to come and get the ring. That he's gonna be buried with it."

I got up, stunned and sobered. Twilight was upon us, with its last streaks of red-and-purple sunset across the freshly planted fields. In the distance candles glowed in the house windows. "Can I write him a note?" I asked. "Is there somehow I can get a message to him? And food?"

"That Captain Wirz ain't gonna 'low no notes or food. You see how he didn't let Mistis bring in supplies today."

I started to walk back to the house.

"Doan you do nuthin' foolish now, Eulinda."

"What would I do?" I asked. "What could I do?"

His answer did not come. For there was no answer. There was only the quiet night, the farm smells, the distant woods and fields holding their secrets and the one-mile distance between me and that prison where Neddy was sealed up.

Maybe forever.

And me here, sleeping in my bed in the house at night and knowing he was there, my only brother, and knowing likely I'd never see him again.

Neddy, starving and dying. To make himself come true.

And to show me that nothing else mattered if you didn't do that.

Well, I resolved, I'll do it too. I'll make myself come true, as Moll said. I don't know how yet. But I'll find a way. I won't let what Neddy is doing be for nothing.

CHAPTER SEVEN

Mr. Julian Writes,
Mr. Hampton Has Another Spell,
and I Learn Why He Wept and
What It Has to Do
With Us

SOMETHING WAS NOT RIGHT ABOUT THE whole thing, and I tossed and turned all night in my bed thinking on what it was.

When I slept it was not with my whole mind. Part of me was always a little awake, a little watchful.

Toward dawn I did sleep, and when I woke I had the answer.

Because when I woke all I could see was Mr. Hampton yesterday, with his hands over his face, weeping.

And then I heard Mistis's voice, as I had that night when I lingered outside the dining room window on the piazza. She was telling him that one of these days he was going to have to put her in charge.

He is not in charge anymore, I told myself. And that is why he was weeping. If he were still in charge, he would go back to the prison and fetch Neddy home.

He would promise him his freedom.

That was what was wrong. Mr. Hampton was no longer in charge. And I would have to find out what was going on.

～◎ ・ ◎～

It was Moll who told me.

That day, with the baby in the house, everything was different. Nobody paid much mind to me. Mistis was fluttering about like a butterfly around Janie and the baby. The rules were put aside and I wandered free, poking around.

As usual, what I wanted to know was just beneath the surface of things. As usual the servants all knew already. And maybe the reason I didn't know was because of the way I was. Namby-pamby, and always willing to trust Mistis and Mr. Hampton, and not actually looking out for what lay in wait behind the bushes to harm me.

And maybe this was what Neddy was trying to teach me.

Moll was washing all the baby clothes that had been sent by neighbors. She had the laundry pot over a fire in back of the kitchen, and she was stirring the water with a battlin' stick.

"How that baby doin'?" she asked.

"Dr. Head says she's in good health."

"Mistis seems awful cosy with that Yankee woman."

"Yes. They're talking about things up North I don't even know about."

"That Yankee woman know about Mistis?"

"Know what?"

"That she owns slaves?"

I caught Moll's eye and knew right off, she wasn't concerned about Janie. What she was asking was if I knew. But what? Whatever it was, it must have just happened, and I'd been too worried about Neddy to understand.

"What are you saying?" I asked her. "What's going on?"

"What makes you think anythin's goin' on?"

"I feel it, Moll. I woke up this morning feeling it. Something is different."

She grunted. "Sure 'nuf is."

"What?"

She cast a look to either side of her, though no one was about. "You remember, couple of days ago when that gentleman come from Atlanta?"

I hadn't paid attention. Again. I hadn't looked for what was lying wait behind the bushes. But I said yes.

"He was a lawyer."

Lawyers are never good. I knew that from Uncle

Phineas's house in Atlanta. Lawyers meant trouble. "What did he want?"

"Let's see if I can 'splain right. The master, he put everythin' in her name. The whole plantation. And all of us. She owns everythin' now."

I felt a wave of shock go through me. Had I dreamed it? Sensed it? "Why?"

"Sancho says the way he heard it, it was so the 'Federacy can't take his property if they think he do treason."

"Treason? What treason?"

She shrugged and set down the battlin' stick. She held her hand over her belly, which was getting rounder every day. "All's I know is we hers now. An' she kin sell us off anytime she wants."

"It's why master was crying last night," I said. And I told her how he cried about Neddy.

"Thas' right," she said. "He oughta cry. He knows he done lost us all. So you better be careful, Eulinda. Doan get on her wrong side. He cain't help you no more."

I wandered off, thinking how he'd told me only a mite before how the day would come when he couldn't help me anymore. And I almost felt sorry for him as I went back to the house.

⊷ · ⊶

That afternoon Mr. Hampton requested that I help him

with one of his experiments. When I got to his study he was seated at a round table in front of the window that overlooked the piazza. On the table was a chessboard, a bottle of ink, a quill pen, and some paper.

"Did you know, Eulinda, that if you put a grain of corn on the first square of the chessboard and double it on every square, by the time you get to the last square you will have four hundred twenty-nine million, nine hundred and thirty-five thousand, eight hundred and ten grains?"

"No, sir, I didn't." But I did know that every time he could not face the world or what was happening, he hid himself in his study, and conducted his experiments.

"It's true," he said gravely. "I have calculated it."

I stood fidgeting, hoping he wasn't going to ask me to help him count the corn grains.

"I would measure your head today, Eulinda," he said.

My head? I became frightened. But he just smiled.

"Nothing to be afraid of. I simply take measurements of your head and determine the placement of your skull bones, then make notations. It's a scientific experiment in the North. How your skull bones are placed indicates character. Come, sit."

So I let him measure my skull, listening to his chatter. The windows in the room were open and the late March air was warm and fragrant. Before we were through, we heard hoofbeats.

"Looks like a post rider from the station," he said.

He went himself to the door, something he would not do if Mistis was about. I heard him talking with the man about the mild weather, then the news.

I heard them say how Sherman was planning an advance soon. Then Mr. Hampton directed him to the kitchen and the well for refreshments for him and water for his horse.

The front door closed, but he did not come back into his study. I heard the rustling of paper from the hall, then a mild, "Oh, oh." Then a gasp.

I ran into the hall. He was on a chair, the three or four papers of the letter in his hand. There was a sheen of perspiration on his brow. "Go and get Dr. Head, Eulinda," he said. "Take Tippo."

◦ ⋅ ◦

I rode as fast as I could. Mr. Hampton had taught me to ride when I was younger, but of late, since the war, I'd not pushed the favor, because the others in the quarters might think I was lording it over them.

But it's not something you forget, riding a horse like Tippo. He sensed the urgency of the situation and did his best, and his best gave me all I could do to hold on.

By the time I got to town, my hair was disheveled, my

skirts up around my thighs, my breath spent, and I looked like the harridan I was.

And I realized how much I loved Mr. Hampton, how much he meant to me.

At Dr. Head's house, his wife pointed to the tavern where Mr. Hampton always played billiards. I tied Tippo and went inside. The dimness blinded me. I smelled cigar smoke and whiskey, heard laughter, and saw the men, six of them, lounging around the billiard table. They looked up when I came in.

"Why it's Kellogg's little girl," one of them said.

Kellogg's little girl. Is that how he spoke of me to them? As his little girl? Is that how he thought of me?

"Everything all right at Pond Bluff, Eulinda?" It was Dr. Head speaking. And I didn't have to answer. Because he knew it wasn't.

⚜ • ⚜

I sat with Mr. Hampton, beside the settee in his study, where he lay. Mistis and Janie were having their supper in the dining room. I heard them talking.

I heard the plain everyday sounds from all over the house, the tall-case clock in the hall, the whirring of Mr. Hampton's under-the-glass clock on his desk, the clatter of pots from the far off kitchen.

Dr. Head had said Mr. Hampton had a more serious

kind of spell. "Pain in the chest," he'd told Mistis. "Giddiness in the head. I have bled the left arm, put poultices on him, and given him camphor and laudanum. He must not become overagitated, Mrs. Kellogg, or one of these spells will get the best of him someday."

"We'll keep him quiet," she promised. "We'll worry him with nothing."

Then she'd told him about the letter from Mr. Julian. It was from Elmira Prison, and he was very sickly.

"I thought a letter would be good for him," she said. "At least he knows now that his son is alive."

"It normally would be," Dr. Head had said, "except that he'd just visited Andersonville. And when he thinks of Julian being sick in a place like that, well, what can I say?"

"Is Elmira as bad, Dr. Head?"

"I don't think so, but try convincing him of that. My advice is, no talk of prisons. If you must, tell him I have personally heard from colleagues up North that Elmira is considerably better than Andersonville."

Lies, lies, I thought, watching him sleep. Everybody's lying to everybody else around here. Nobody can stand the truth, any of it. Then, as I sat looking at Mr. Hampton's pale face, fear coursed through me. What if he died?

He was the one around here who held us all together, even if he didn't legally run things anymore. Somehow I knew, like I'd known the other morning upon waking, that things were different.

His presence alone kept Mistis civil to us. His presence kept her decent. If he died, she would give in to all her evil. She'd sell us all off, sell this place off, and go back to Atlanta with her brother.

Please don't let him die, I prayed. He is the only thing that stands between all of us and terror.

"Your head, Eulinda." He woke then. He was smiling at me.

"Sir?"

"I was taking the measurements of your head. That's the last thing I remember. The measurements told me that you have excellent character. You are honest, and brave, and true."

I could not trust myself to speak. I clutched his hand. He closed his eyes and went back to sleep again. And I thought, Oh, Mr. Hampton, I'm not, I'm not. But I want to be. Is wanting to be, enough? I would find out in the weeks to come.

⋘ . ⋙

Things settled down. The baby and Janie became part of the household. The corn and potatoes and cotton and grain grew in the fields. Mr. Hampton got better and spent the fine spring afternoons on the piazza. Sometimes

I sat and read to him. Sometimes he even rode Tippo around the plantation to check on the fields.

Roper and Homer came home from their work at the prison, and one night I sat around with everyone in Moll and Sancho's cabin and heard Roper tell how "Dey got a whole town in that prison now, wif' street names like Broadway an' South Street an' Water Street. An' de prisoners do bizness. One be a tailor, 'nother cut hair, and others cook fer them what has money to pay. An' dat Captain Wirz, I see him shoot a prisoner fer no reason."

Mistis set Roper and Homer to work building a false floor in the corn crib to hide her good silver if the Yankees came.

"But you're a Yankee," I heard Roper tell her. It was early morning, and she was out there overseeing the work and his voice carried in the air, a question unanswered.

She spoke to him sharply. So he finished the false floor. Then she had them dig a secret root cellar in the bluffs near the pond, where she would hide hams and chicken and cheese.

Spring came in full force and nobody paid mind to the prison anymore. At least nobody spoke of it.

And then one day, near the end of April, I had a conversation with Janie Hunt, and she invited me to go North with her.

CHAPTER EIGHT

How I'm Invited to Go North and Refuse, and End Up Doing Something to Help Janie

SHE WAS SITTING UNDER THE ARBOR IN Mistis's garden, knitting something for the baby, who was lying on some bedding on the grass. She invited me to come sit with her.

"I'm given to understand you are Mr. Kellogg's daughter." She said it right off. Nothing namby-pamby about her.

I sat on the bench next to her. "Who told you that?"

"Oh, I've spoken with some of the servants. You are a pretty child."

"I'm not a child," I said.

"Oh, forgive me. I shouldn't say such. I know with this war childhood has been denied to many. Or should I say"—and she gave me a careful look—"that slavery denies childhood. Is that it?"

"You could say that."

"You've been educated. You speak well. May I assume you also read and write?"

I said yes.

"And you have a brother in the prison camp. My husband is still there, you know. Though in better straits than your brother. He's been made a ward master in the prison hospital, which means he can get outside the grounds. I expect him to come and see us someday." She gave a little laugh.

But it was a nervous laugh. "Run away?" I asked.

"Thirteen have run in the month of April. Word came to Homer and Toomy."

"You've been speaking to Homer and Toomy?"

"To all the servants."

Something here. I made myself alert. No more would I be harmed from something hiding behind the bushes. "Some have," I said. "But they have a Mr. Harris there, who goes after them with dogs."

She was silent for a minute before speaking again. "Up North I'm an Abolitionist," she said.

"And here?"

"Well, one doesn't let geography change one's moral

views. You seem cast down. I've been watching you. I imagine that being Mr. Kellogg's daughter is a confusing lot. You are neither this nor that. Or are you?" She looked at me.

"I'm a house servant," I said.

"You're a slave. In bondage, then."

"Yes."

"Are you happy with things the way they are?"

I shook my head, no. "I used to be, when I was a child. But as I said, I'm not a child anymore."

There was another spell of silence. Then she spoke very softly. "I could get you North. Would you like to go North with me?"

I stared at her.

"Your mistress has secured me and my baby passage on a blockade runner taking a load of cotton North. It seems she and her brother have an interest in it. Trouble is, it leaves out of the port of New Orleans. And because my family is well placed, I can make other arrangements. Would you like to come with me?"

I continued staring, taking it all in. Because her family was well placed! And she not yet twenty! How I envied her assurance, the way she knew her place in the world!

"How would that be possible?" I asked. "Mistis would never let me go."

She smiled. "There are ways. Well, would you like to?"

I thought for a minute. The idea was so strange. Walk off from everything I knew? Was that the way I was to make myself come true? It's one way, I told myself, but not the only way.

"I thank you," I told her, though I don't know where the words or the thoughts came from. It was as if they were in me, waiting to come out, waiting to be said, so I could know my own mind.

"I thank you, and it isn't that I want to stay here. Or that I'm afraid. But there are things I must do here, before I leave. I don't mean on this plantation. But here, in this part of the country."

"What things?" she asked.

I knew she was thinking, What things could a little slave girl possibly do? "I don't know yet," I told her. "I just know I can't leave just yet, is all."

She nodded. "I know you're not afraid. You have inner strength and purpose. I can see it in the way you hold yourself, in your eyes."

"You can?" I asked, disbelieving.

"Yes. So I would ask you to help me."

"Help you?"

She nodded. "I do not understand Mrs. Kellogg, nor do I hope to. She has been kind to me, taking me and my baby in, so I must try not to judge her. You see, I can't leave here and go home without my husband. The blockade runner leaves in two weeks, which means my baby and I will be taken, by carriage, to Atlanta, next week. Mrs. Kellogg is having us driven there. It would be such a simple matter, once the carriage leaves this place, to meet my husband somewhere near here. If he were to slip away from the prison. And someone were to meet him in the woods and tell him where to meet us."

I nodded, listening. She was asking me to be the someone. "Who's driving the carriage?" I asked.

"A man named Sancho."

"You'll be safe with him."

"I know. I've already spoken with him. It was he who suggested you."

"Sancho said I might help?"

"Yes. He said you're allowed the freedom to roam the area and often do. And you were angry enough about things to help."

I nodded, and smiled to myself. Then I said. "Sancho knows me a long time. He's right. When do you want to do it?"

～⊙ · ⊙～

And so it was that a week later I found myself making my way through the familiar fields on a misty morning. I was on my way to find Captain Henry Hunt. Over my shoulder was a sack with some biscuits and ham, still warm from breakfast, for Captain Hunt.

Over the last couple of days, I had taken a pair of trousers from Mr. Julian's old room, and a pair of boots. Secretly, Janie had sewn her husband a new shirt.

The evening before Janie had made her farewells to Mistis and Mr. Hampton. They slept late, knowing that she would be leaving at first light this morning. It had been arranged that Iris was to pack her a repast in a picnic basket. In her reticule she had a letter of introduction to people in a safe house in Atlanta, people known to Mistis and Uncle Phineas. Only, those people wouldn't tell Uncle Phineas Janie's husband was with her, because they were also friends of Janie's, unknown to Mistis and Uncle Phineas. Nor would they tell that Janie would leave from Atlanta and not New Orleans. I often got up early and wandered about the place, so there was nothing to arouse suspicion about any of the doings of the morning.

Nobody would be in any trouble. Unless I got caught that morning.

In the mist, every tree looked like a witch to me, or a haint. Every sound was Mr. Harris and his dogs. But I didn't care. It was about time I did something of worth, something to start me on my way to making myself true.

The sound of the nearby creek was like the roar of a river. Or was it the sound of my own blood pounding in my ears?

In some places the mist was so thick I couldn't see six feet in front of me.

I was to meet Captain Hunt on the curve in the creek. He knew to go west after leaving the south gate of the prison. But he didn't know where to meet his wife and baby, because after the creek, he didn't know the landscape.

I did. I was to take him, in the woods, to a place about a mile from the peach orchard on Pond Bluff. There, at a dip in the road, Sancho would stop to check a wheel on the wagon, at about seven o'clock. In the wagon, Sancho had built a false floor, a space big enough for Captain Hunt to lie down in until they were at the safe house in Atlanta.

I'd left the house at six. I knew it took only fifteen minutes to get to the bend in the creek. And I was properly terrified. But only for about five minutes, when I crossed an open field. Then I laughed at myself. How often in the past had I run through this field on my way to check my traps?

Who could prove I was doing anything else?

So I ran, thinking what Janie had said, about thirteen

escaping from the prison in April. Some had hidden in ration barrels, some had clung to the bottom of ration wagons, some had pretended to be dead, some had tunneled their way out, others had scaled the wall when the nights were foggy. And some had just walked away from a work detail, like Captain Hunt.

The signal was to be two calls of the whippoorwill, given by Captain Hunt, when he saw me clear the open field and take shelter in the trees by the creek. As I knelt down in the wet underbrush, hearing the beating of my own heart, the sound came.

I heard his scuffling and breathing before I saw him. Then I smelled him, the creek smell on him, earthy and fishy.

"Eulinda?"

"Yes. Captain Hunt?"

"The same, thank God. Have you seen anyone or been followed?"

"No sir. You?"

"Nothing so far. I've not yet been missed, but we must hurry."

We stuck to the creek until we reached where it gave us a view of Pond Bluff in the distance. We hid behind trees and ran bent over when there were none. Then, when we were in the spot where the Peach Orchard met the creek, we made for the dusty road that led, eventually, to Atlanta.

"Only a mile more," I told him.

When we reached the spot in the road where the wagon would stop, it was not there yet. Captain Hunt had a pocket watch. It was only quarter of seven, so we crouched down in the woods and waited.

I gave him some biscuits with ham in them, still warm from breakfast. He ate them ravenously. "God bless you, child, I haven't had such food in months."

I had a good look at him then. His hair was reddish brown and long. He had no beard. His nose was sharp, his eyes blue. He even had some freckles across his face. He was young, no more than twenty-five. His clothing was ragged but reasonably clean.

"I washed in the hospital," he said. "Used strong soap. No lice, no bugs. I wanted to be clean for my wife and baby."

"Janie brought you clothes," I told him. "And you look about the right size for them."

He put a hand on my arm. "I'm beholden to you, Eulinda," he said. "I wish there was something I could have done to get your brother out. But he's inside, as I told Toomy and Homer in my message, and I come out on work detail."

I didn't say Neddy didn't want to come anyway. I just said yes, I understood. And that it was great sport helping him.

It was. Smuggling the clothing, fetching the food that morning, and knowing Janie was sewing that shirt in secret at night in her room had been exciting and all too easy.

Now this seemed too easy, also. But I had no qualms. Hadn't all those thirteen who escaped in April made it?

Then we heard wagon wheels, the snorting of a horse, the jingling of a harness, and grinned at each other. His teeth, I noticed, were still good. He must have managed to get food in prison. And I wondered about Neddy and remembered what beautiful teeth he'd had.

The wagon came into sight. And sure enough it stopped. I heard Sancho's voice. "Just wanna check that wheel, Miss Janie."

I saw, through the branches of some bushes, Sancho squatting down to check the wheel, saw him take off his hat and glance into the woods. That was the signal, the taking off of the hat. It meant they hadn't seen anybody on the road, hadn't been followed.

"Well, good-bye, Eulinda," Captain Hunt said. "Thank you again, child. You'd best get right home. And when you're ready to come North, get in touch with us. Did

Janie give you our address?"

I said yes. Then, in one quick motion he hugged and kissed me. "God bless," he said. And he ran, still crouching to the wagon.

I saw when I looked again that Sancho already had the false floor open. I saw him and Janie in a quick embrace. I saw him kiss the baby, then climb in to lie down.

I waited until they got on their way again. I waved to Janie as they passed, but I don't know if she saw me.

⋙ • ⋘

They sent some sour-faced men to Pond Bluff the next day to ask after Captain Hunt. Mistis was taken by surprise, and her surprise worked for her. "Why, I sent his wife and baby off to Atlanta just the other day to friends," she told them. "I never saw the man."

"You wouldn't be funnin' us now, would you?" one of them asked her. "Takin' that woman in so's you kin help her and her husband run off?"

"I assure you, gentlemen, everything is aboveboard. I have no wish to anger the Confederate authorities. Captain Wirz was looking for a neighbor to take her off his hands, and I merely obliged him."

"He musta followed her to Atlanta." That was their conclusion.

"Gentlemen, if my wife says she had nothing to do

with it, she had nothing to do with it," Mr. Hampton told them. Thank heaven he was having a good day.

Nobody asked the servants about anything. And Sancho and I never spoke of it.

〜◦ . ◦〜

I started working in the kitchen regular-like with the approach of summer. Moll was getting near her time, and Iris was trying to take her place in the fields and cook, too. I told Iris I could do the cooking. I wanted time away from the house, time to think, and Mistis didn't object.

"It's about time you made yourself useful around here," she said, "with Moll's lying-in coming close."

I thought a lot as I cut up potatoes, fried bacon, and even made syllabub.

I had thought that helping Captain Hunt and Janie make their escape would make me feel like I was making myself come true. But it didn't. I didn't feel any better about myself than I had before. Which meant only one thing. There was something else I had to do to make myself come true. Only I didn't know what it was.

All right, Miss Brave I-Don't-Want-to-Go-North, I told myself. What are you going to do now?

I peeled a lot of potatoes, fried a lot of bacon, and cooked up a whole mess of chickens in the months that followed, and still I didn't find out.

CHAPTER NINE

How the Months Went By, I Became a Cook, and Mr. Lincoln's "Great Measure" Came to Pond Bluff

IN MAY MR. HAMPTON CAME INTO THE kitchen after his breakfast one morning and told me that Confederate cavalry officer Jeb Stuart had been mortally wounded at a place called Yellow Tavern in Virginia.

"It's a great loss to the South," he told me.

I said yessir and went on with my work. He sat down at the table and I offered him more tea. He sat and told me about his latest experiment. He was interested in people's fingers, the ends of their fingers. "You can put black ink on them and press them on paper and every person is different," he told me.

Then he told me I would be a fine cook someday.

"Yessir, I'd like to be."

"The war will be over one of these days, and it is our

obligation to prepare our people to take their place in the world."

I went along with the lie. He knew I was in the kitchen to get away from Mistis. I knew he missed me. It was sad and confusing, and neither one of us knew what to do about it.

He started coming to the kitchen every morning after finishing breakfast with Mistis. He'd sit and talk.

So I'd give him a cup of tea. And he'd give me intelligence about what was happening with the war.

In late May, he told me that Sherman's men were as far South as Marietta.

In June he said, "Did I forget to mention that Abraham Lincoln was nominated for a second term?"

He expected no replies from me. At first I thought it was just idle chatter, but it wasn't before long that I minded that he wanted me to know these things. And to share them with the other slaves.

In June Moll had her baby. A little boy. In July I gave Mr. Hampton cold lemonade, for it was very, very hot. He told me how disappointed he was that Annalee had not been to see him when he had had his last spell.

One day in August he did not come. And Iris told us that he'd gone to Atlanta on business, and I worried about him in Atlanta in the summertime.

In August it rained a lot and all the roads turned into a red mud. When he finally did come back to the kitchen in September, it was to tell me that Atlanta had fallen.

"I'd like to locate Julian one day," he told me.

He had written to Julian but no more letters had come. He never spoke the words, but I knew he thought Julian was dead.

"Many refugees from Atlanta will be coming South," he said. "Some might find their way to Pond Bluff. If they do, they are to be well treated."

"And what of Annalee?" I asked. "And Uncle Phineas?"

"They will be safe. He is, after all, a Yankee. And she is under his protection."

But then one day Mistis came into the kitchen, stood there looking around, and spoke to me. "I am fixing up the room you sleep in for Annalee. In case she comes home now that Atlanta has fallen."

"But she has her own room," I said.

"A young girl of her station needs her own parlor, to receive her own friends when they come. I am fixing your room up as a parlor for her," she told me.

"Yes, ma'am."

"Kindly remove your things by tonight."

She did not say where I was to sleep. I moved into the

cabin Iris lived in. She had room. I moved back to the quarters.

This is where I belong, I told myself my first night there, after Iris had covered me with a light quilt. This is where I came from and this is where I belong. When the Yankees come they should find me here. Not upstairs in the big house in a featherbed. This is where Neddy should find me, too.

For I am the sister of Zeke, who was sold south. And I have been untrue to all of them. This is where I belong.

But I cried myself to sleep anyway.

In November Mr. Hampton came to the kitchen and told me how Abraham Lincoln had been reelected, and how Captain Wirz was sending some prisoners away from Andersonville to other prisons in the South, lest Sherman's cavalry pay a visit.

He said not a word about my moving to the quarters. He stepped around that subject like he would have stepped around a mess of broken eggs on the floor.

It was a wet and cold winter. The walls of Iris's cabin let the air in. She moved my bed near the hearth. I thought how lucky I was to have a shelter over my head and a bed and a hearth, when the prisoners at Andersonville had none of these things.

On Christmas Day I went to the big house with the

others to receive presents from Mr. Hampton. He gave every servant a new pair of shoes, some warm trousers for the men, and new warm shifts for the women. He gave out plenty of rum. I wore my oldest calico dress, the one that was too short, with the frayed hem and the patched skirt. I saw Mr. Hampton's eyes go over me, saw the pain in them, and thought, Good. I am no longer going to hide what I am. This is what I am, and if you want to remedy it you must do something. And not keep letting her have her way.

But he did nothing.

I knew that Mr. Hampton and Mistis had taken a wagonload of home remedies and vegetables at Christmas for the prisoners. The day after Christmas he came to the kitchen and told me the prison guards were without shoes, shivering atop their pigeon-roost sentry towers in the bone-chilling cold.

On New Year's Day he and Mistis had callers. Annalee was coming to visit, finally, with some friends from school. Uncle Phineas was bringing them.

I went with Boy-Jack to the dining room to start the fire in the hearth. I was wearing the same dress I'd worn on Christmas Day, for I'd been working hard, collecting kindling, and carrying meat up from the springhouse.

While Boy-Jack was starting the fire, I looked around

at the elegance of the house. The lush draperies and furniture, the gleaming silver and cut crystal, made me dizzy. Everything seemed to close in on me. I had once lived here, not in Iris's mean, bare-floored cabin.

Possessions aren't important, I told myself. But once you've lived in a house, its lines, its rooms, and what's in them furnish your heart.

On my way out, the guests were just arriving. I tried to dash out back to the dogtrot, but Uncle Phineas called me from the front of the hall. "Eulinda, is that you?"

I turned and curtsied. "Yessir."

He removed his tall hat and walked toward me in his shining boots and tweed jacket. "Child, what has happened to you?"

He'd always been good to me. "Nothing, sir. I was helping out, is all."

His eyes went over me. I had once stood in his parlor and recited some Shakespeare for him. I saw understanding in his eyes. He sighed and smiled. "My sister must be having some Confederates to dinner," he said. "It's shameful what we True Yankees have to do to hide our good works from the Rebels, isn't it?"

I agreed that it was, yes. Shameful.

Next day Mr. Hampton came to the kitchen for his tea. He told me not to venture too far from the house, that the woods were filling up with Confederate deserters and war refugees.

"People are living in abandoned railroad cars and under bridges. This thing is almost over, Eulinda."

In February, all the slaves on the plantation started talking about the end of the war and what they would do. "We gonna have to git married agin," Sancho told Moll. "I heard that these Nigra marriages doan hold up in court."

"Who says I wanna marry you agin?" Moll asked, even as she held her eight-month-old baby boy in her arms.

"First Yankee soldier what comes through, I'm goin' wif' him," said Boy-Jack.

Toomy waved his one good hand. "What kin I do? I'll stay right here."

Iris said she'd put her belongings in a scarf on her head and just start walkin' west. Man-Jack said likely he'd stay here, too. The others mocked him.

"What you gonna do, Eulinda?" they asked me.

"Wait for Neddy. Or go to the prison and look for him."

At the end of February Mr. Hampton told me that Wilmington, North Carolina, had fallen. In March we all knew the end was coming. The servants got restless, put down their hoes early in the day, took things from the springhouse without fear of punishment. Two fields remained unplowed. You could feel the change in the air, the waiting, and the ending of things.

In April Mr. Hampton came to the kitchen. "I wish you to go to the quarters and summon everyone," he said. "I have something to tell them."

So it had come, then. A strange quiet lay over the place. Where was everybody? I felt eyes watching me. I saw a hawk circling lazily over the fields. At my feet Otis scurried around and barked at nothing.

They were all in their cabins. I stood in the dirt path in the middle of the quarters and yelled, "Mr. Hampton said he got something important to tell us!"

They knew what it was, of course. Hadn't they waited for it for years? Doors opened. They stepped out cautiously, all afraid that if they didn't behave proper-like, it would go away.

"Come on," I said to them. "Come on right along with me. Up to the piazza. It's the day you've all been waiting for."

I felt like the only grown-up, leading a group of children, and I thought, I'm the one chosen to do this, like I'm a messenger from Mr. Hampton, like I'm still part of them at the house.

But I was too happy for everybody to think much on that. Quietly they came with me, and quietly they stood waiting, until the front door opened, and Mr. Hampton and Mistis came out.

I stood with the slaves and waited. I took my place beside them, not the Kelloggs. I knew where I belonged.

Mistis had a Bible in her hands. Mr. Hampton took off his hat and looked us all over.

"You all are free now," he said. "The war is over. You're just as free as I am. And there are some things I want to tell you."

Everyone stood still and respectful, as if they were being told what work to do this day. And before he spoke again, tears came down Mr. Hampton's cheeks.

"Eulinda," he said, "I've raised you since you were a baby. You too, Boy-Jack, and you're almost a man. Since you were a boy, I've tried to be good to you and take good care of all of you in return for the good work you all have always done for me. I want you all to go out into the world now and make good citizens. Be honest and respectable, and don't turn against the good raisin' you have had, and remember me and my wife love you all."

Still nobody moved.

"It is not an easy world out there. If you get into trouble, come to me and I will help you. As for me, I need help on this place, to plow and to plant, just as always. If any of you want to work for me, I shall pay you. If not, well, then, you may go."

Behind me I heard some amens, some whispered praising of God, but no more. Then the master, eyes dimmed with tears, turned and went back into the house. And she did, too.

And that's how the end of the war and Mr. Lincoln's great measure come to Pond Bluff.

CHAPTER TEN

What the Prison Looked Like Empty, and How I Met Mr. Griffin and Made One of My First Decisions as a Free Woman

ON A MORNING IN MAY I WAS WANDERING through the fields with Otis when he sighted a figure on the road and started barking. A lone man was standing there, wearing what looked like the remnants of a Confederate uniform.

There had been no Confederate uniforms in this area since April, when Yankee cavalry had overrun the place. I'd come twice since the prison closed to stare in the great open front gate. I'd see the dust from inside the stockade swirling around the debris and the remains of the old shebangs of the prisoners. Some were made out of old shirts or trousers, and they'd be propped up on sticks and flapping in the breeze, ghostly reminders of those who had made them.

I'd go up the hill to the cemetery and see pigs rooting

around in there. I'd shiver at the scene, wondering if I had the mettle to go in and look for Neddy.

I knew he was dead. If he were alive he'd have come to Pond Bluff to get me. I'd see the bones sticking up from the ground where the rain had washed the earth away. And I'd see the rats scampering about over everything.

On the plantation everyone except Toomy and Man-Jack had left. Mr. Hampton was holed up in his study, fooling around with fingerprints. He was now retrieving everything of Julian's and insisting he could find his son's fingermarks on them.

Mistis ran the place. She had hired wage servants to plant and work. Though there was not a bit of currency left in all of Georgia that was worth anything, Mistis had money. All the crops were doing well, and she had purchased six new horses from the Yankees.

At home I ran the kitchen, cooked their meals. I lived in Iris's cabin and Mistis paid me three dollars a month.

I decided to go over to the road and see who the man was in the Confederate uniform.

❧ · ❧

"Hello," I said.

He was tall, over six feet, with a good span of shoulders. He had the bearing of an officer, though neither his coat nor his hat had any fancy furberlows to tell his rank.

The coat was open in front, and the shirt under it was clean. All of his clothes were faded and patched. A pair of old, mustard-colored gloves were shoved into his belt, and his horse was glossy, and middling well fed, and on the blanket it said CSA. He was no outrider, no vagrant. He had a woman to see after him.

He was not old in years. But when I saw his eyes, I knew that he would never be young again.

He nodded. He had a mustache that drooped down and sideburns, but no beard, heavy stern brows, and a rugged nose.

The horse hung its head near his shoulder. You could see they were a pair, had been for a while. They spoke of it in their silences.

"My name's Eulinda. I live near here. You come to find somebody in there?"

"A lot of somebodies," he said. He held out his hand. Otis licked it, so I knew right off he was a man of good parts. Otis never would have any truck with anybody who wasn't. Then he ruffled Otis's head and ears, the way a man will do with a dog.

"I swan," I said, "he likes you. That's strange. Ever since they took him inside that place once, he's hated any sight of a uniform."

He raised his eyebrows. "Took him inside?"

"A guard did. Said he was going to sell him to the Yankees. My master, leastways he was then, got him back, though."

"Where is the man who was your master now?"

"Back home. In his study. Trying to get his dead son's fingermarks off his books and things. His son is missing in the war."

"That so?"

"Yessir. And Mr. Hampton's got no more sap in him anymore, it seems."

"You're free now, though."

"Yessir."

"But you didn't leave Mr. Hampton?"

"Most of the others left, but I'm not ready yet."

He looked at me again. "You speak very well."

"Mistis educated me."

He nodded and sighed, looking back again at the open gate. "What a confused mess. We'll straighten it out though. All we need is time." Then he stuck out his hand. "My name is William Griffin. From Fort Valley, a bit north. I heard about this place. Had to come and see for myself if it was as bad as they say."

I shook hands with him. Never had I shaken hands with anyone before in my life! And him a Confederate officer! "Well, is it?" I asked.

He sighed. "It's worse. Makes me ashamed, is what it does. And I promised myself I'd never be ashamed of what I did for the Confederacy. Sure, we got beat. But that's nothing to be ashamed of. This is."

We both stood looking in silence for a bit. Finally, I spoke. "My brother is in there."

"Oh, so that's the way of it. He ran off and joined the Yankee army, did he?"

"Yessir. Eighth United States Colored Troops."

"Are you here then to give your brother a proper burial?"

"Yessir."

"Well, Eulinda, I've come to do just that."

I stared at him. "Bury my brother?"

"Bury them all proper-like. Clean this place up. I heard from some local blacks that the graves are being uprooted by animals. And looters are stealing every pane of glass or piece of metal left. I aim to set that place right."

"All by yourself?"

"If need be."

"But you're a Confederate officer."

"That's part of why I aim to do it, Eulinda. That and because no decent man, Confederate or Yankee, ought to be able to let such conditions as this abide."

"I'll help you," I said. I don't know what made me say it, but I felt drawn to this tall man with the sideburns, the soldier's way about him, and the sad eyes.

"I'll pay you," he said. "Out of my own pocket. And if you know any other Negroes who are willing to help, tell them I'll pay them, too."

I nodded and moved away. "When you want to start, Mister?"

"Tomorrow morning. Be here nine sharp. And bring any others with you."

※ · ※

I got Toomy and Man-Jack to come and help, too. When I told them about it, that Mr. Griffin was paying, they put down their hoes and came right along with me the next morning.

I made breakfast for Mr. Hampton and Mistis as always. Only before I took my leave, I decided to tell them what I was about. It seemed only proper.

"Ma'am, I won't be here to serve your noon meal. I'm going to work for Mr. Griffin."

She set down her coffee cup. "And who, pray, is Mr. Griffin?"

"He used to be an officer in the Confederate army. He's come to set right the graveyard in the prison. He's asked for Negroes to help. I'm going. So are Toomy and Man-Jack."

The cup clattered into her saucer. "Well, who will make our noon dinner? And supper?"

I wanted to say "Maybe you should try." I'd heard that over to Peach Grove Mrs. Hutchinson was doing the cooking. But all I did say was, "Ma'am, I'm leaving cold vittles in the larder for your noon dinner. There's fresh biscuits and cake. I'll be back to fix supper, though it might be a tad late."

"Did you hear that, Hampton?" She turned to him. "Did you ever hear such twaddle? She's your daughter. Speak to her!"

Mr. Hampton had been reading his newspaper. He looked up. "Hey? What is it, dear? I read here that James Wilson is commanding officer of the Union garrison in Macon."

"I said speak to your daughter, Hampton."

"Wilson is setting up quarters at the Lanier Hotel. We ought to pay him a visit, dear. You should be rewarded for your services as a Unionist."

He patted me on the shoulder when I served him more tea. "Good girl," he said, "I knew you'd stay when the others all left."

Mistis slammed down her linen napkin. "Very well, Eulinda, if that's all the thanks I get for everything I have done for you! Go and work for Mr. Griffin. But supper had better be on the table, or you may go and live at the prison!"

Mr. Griffin had a tent set up under some trees the next morning. I approached with Toomy and Man-Jack.

He still wore the uniform, and he had pen and ink, and a paper on which there were some drawings.

"Sir, do you remember me?"

He stood up and was very polite to Toomy and Man-Jack. "What happened to your hand?" he asked Toomy.

"Lost it at the munitions factory in Macon, sir. But I kin work good."

"I have no doubt. Well, here I've made drawings of the place. Here is the stockade"—he pointed with his pen—"and here is the cemetery. The old hospital tents are here. You two, I'd like you to help me clean up in the inside of the stockade this morning. Eulinda, I'm wondering if there are any ledger books around this place anywhere, that will tell us about the graveyard. There ought to be a record of the dead. If you could search the outbuildings and the hospital tents, please."

"Yessir. But later, could I go into the cemetery to look for my brother's grave?"

"No place for a girl now," he said. "There will be time for that."

He gave us gloves to wear to protect our hands. And made us wrap cloths around our faces in case we went near anything that might carry disease. I watched as he, Toomy, and Man-Jack went off toward the stockade bearing shovels and brooms. Then I started toward the hospital tents.

They were just beyond the southeast wall. Some of the canvas was tattered and some loose and all of it filthy dirty. I went inside.

There were no cots. The ground was strewn with dirty old pine needles and straw. It smelled of old urine and a dozen other unsavory things. I saw some filthy bandages in a far corner, and then a small book on the floor, its pages rattling in the mild May morning breeze, and I picked my way through the debris under my feet.

I picked up the book. Here was a diary of sorts! I looked around quickly, to determine if anything else of worth was in the place, then ran out into the fresh air to read it. *I have scurvy,* the open page read.

> *My legs have begun to twist wrongside out, and feet to change in front, and troublesome otherways. My gums swollen and rotting, sloughing off, leaving the teeth ready to rot. My limbs, from the knees to toes, are swollen nearly to bursting, black-purple in color, holes in which the finger can be inserted over an inch, putrid, disgusting*

to look at, while from the knees up, my body is skin and bone, my skin drawn like a parchment on a frame.

Another page said, simply *I am hungry.* Still another read:

There are only fifteen surgeons to treat over 2,000 of us sick. And we with the most terrible diseases: diarrhea, dysentry, hospital gangrene, scurvy. Even here in the hospital we get only a half pint of raw meal, or indigestible cornbread with chunks of the corn cob yet in it, or a mixture of swamp water and coarse cornmeal. They call it soup.

I took the handkerchief off my face. I took off the gloves. I felt a dizziness come over me, reading the diary, as if I were holding the secrets of the dead.

The sun was already high in the sky. I wondered what the bake house would be like. I headed toward it, anxious to find something to busy my hands with. Maybe I could rustle up some vittles for the men. And then, as I approached it, I heard chickens clucking.

They were behind the bake house, wandering and pecking. I went into the dilapidated henhouse and, to my surprise, found some feed. The Confederates had left it. If there are chickens, there are eggs, I told myself. And sure enough, there were. I collected them, lots of them, and decided to make some food for us all. I'd use the bake house. Everything was left as if it had just been used that morning.

When I went home that night I was exhausted, but happy. I had spent my first real day as a free woman, and I liked it.

CHAPTER ELEVEN

Why Mr. Griffin Did Not Have Furbelows on His Uniform, and How I Ran into Trouble with Mistis Again and Learned That Miss Barton Was Coming

"MR. GRIFFIN, SIR, WHY DO YOU STILL WEAR your uniform?"

We two were left at a table under his tent, after the noon meal I'd made of eggs in the bake house.

"My other clothes don't fit me, Eulinda. I lost a lot of weight in the war."

"Then why doesn't it have the furbelows that tell your rank?"

He laughed, a harsh, short sound. "I'm permitted to wear my uniform by the Yankees, but not with any of the furbelows that tell of rank."

I knew he would say no more, so I kept my mouth shut. He had secrets. All men who'd been to war did, that's what Man-Jack had told me. "You doan ask those secrets," he'd said. "'Cause they never gonna tell."

"When can I go to the cemetery?" I asked.

"The cemetery has a serious drainage problem. The rainwater makes long puddles between the rows of graves. We need drainage ditches. I'm bringing in more Negroes. I don't like to ask you, Eulinda. I know it's not what you came here for. But until I get better organized, can you make a noon meal for the workers every day?"

No, it wasn't what I'd come for. But I said yes.

"Good. We'll have to build a kiln to bake our own bricks to put in the sides and the bottoms of the drainage ditches."

I wanted to ask him why he was doing all this, with no authority and out of his own money. Then I supposed he was making up for things that he'd done in the war.

"All men from the war got things they gotta make up fer," Man-Jack told me when I spoke to him about it. "You doan ask. They ain't gonna talk 'bout it, ever. You think if Mr. Julian comes home he gonna talk?"

"I'd just like to see him come home," I said. "Maybe Mr. Hampton would come back in his senses."

"Some men, they ain't never gonna come home," Man-Jack told me. "Some doan wanna. They glad to be lost. Thas' what I heered."

So I listened when Mr. Griffin wanted to tell about the drainage ditch which was so important to him. That was the least I could do for him. And then I showed him the diary I'd found. He said I might keep it.

One afternoon I found blackberries in the woods. Mr. Griffin purchased butter, milk, and flour from some peddlers who came around. They didn't have coffee, so the next day I brought some coffee from Mistis's kitchen. I was able to make blackberry pies.

By the end of the first week Mr. Griffin had a dozen Negroes from the surrounding area working for him. I knew some of them by sight if not by name. Some finished cleaning out the stockade. Others he set to making a kiln to bake bricks. The workers mixed the red Georgia clay with water, put it into molds to dry, then put the bricks into the kiln.

It was hard work. But by the middle of the second week they had lined the trenches in the cemetery with the bricks. The next step, Mr. Griffin told us, was to put the cemetery to order. I felt my heart pounding hard. Maybe now I would find Neddy.

⚓ • ⚓

Already, I was in trouble at home. I'd been late for starting supper twice.

"Do you expect me to sit around here and wait for my

supper," Mistis asked, "while you work for someone else? And I supply your everyday needs? Just what are you doing there, anyway?"

"Pulling weeds," I said. "Raking. Helping to burn debris. Sometimes I cook in the bake house. But there's another Negro man who cooks, too."

"Slave work," she said. "You're free now and you do slave work. Is that what Mr. Lincoln's great measure did for you?"

But it's for something, I wanted to say. And I choose to do it. And I am paid. I am leading my own life, not being bossed around.

I knew she wouldn't understand, so I did not answer. Still I knew something had to be done. I could not keep up with two jobs. At night when I fell onto my little cot in Iris's cabin, my head and body ached with fatigue. I was hard put to get up in the morning for breakfast. And I caught the sad looks of Mr. Hampton many times.

The second week of my working for Mr. Griffin, a note arrived from General Wilson, saying he'd heard of the work being done there and was coming to see it for himself. He'd be there in two days.

So there wasn't much time to think of my problem. General James Wilson was the commander of all the Yankee forces in Georgia. We had to make ready for him.

Mr. Griffin gathered us together and talked to us. "This man is United States Cavalry," he said. "He slashed through Alabama, then took this prison. He's the only Yankee who could rout our General Nathan Forrest. He's seen this prison at its worst. So he'll know what's been done already. But there is still more to do."

So we worked ourselves to the bone for the next two days. The weeds outside the gates were cut. Mr. Griffin had the men salvage all the lumber they could and start to build a fence around the cemetery. I helped gather the lumber.

The cemetery was fifty acres. They could not half finish. But it was started. And then General Wilson and his men arrived at the appointed time, and Mr. Griffin took them around to see what all had been done.

The others were talking amongst themselves, but I saw Mr. Griffin and General Wilson standing up on the dirt road in the graveyard. The afternoon sun slanted through the scraggly trees. They stood alone, talking, one in shabby gray, the other in dandified blue, and I wondered what they were talking about.

What could they have to say to each other? Perhaps it could be said only in a graveyard.

Presently they came down the dirt road and Mr. Griffin brought the general over. "These are the people who did all the work," he said. "They've been tireless. They deserve the credit, not me. They're good workers."

None of us had ever seen a Yankee general before, much less one that had slashed through Alabama.

He was tall and wore a mustache and short beard. He was a stern-looking man. His eyes were made of blue steel. They alone could have routed General Forrest. And his uniform had all the furbelows.

How blue it is, I thought. How polished his buttons are. Oh yes, he looks like someone who could rout Forrest.

His horses were smartly turned out, too. Their harnesses and saddles were all polished. On the blankets it said USA. I had never seen that in my lifetime, and I felt a strange thrill go through me. The wonder of it, I thought. Here in this desolate place, the bright beautiful horses of the Yankee army. And its men, so trained, with an aura of confidence and rightness.

General Wilson thanked us and shook the hand of each one in turn. The other Negroes were taken with his manner. I believe no one had ever thanked them for anything in their lives. Or shaken their hands.

One elderly Negro had tears coming down his face when Wilson thanked him.

Then General Wilson turned to Mr. Griffin. "I have

the authority to make you superintendent of this place," he said. "I have no authority to pay the Negro workers, however."

"I pay them," Mr. Griffin said.

"Good. I can offer you a salary. And I will send supplies and rations to help feed your workers."

I thought I saw tears in Mr. Griffin's eyes. And I thought, this is what I am doing here, Mistis. This.

☙ · ❧

Every day I took home with me the smell from that place, which was like no smell I'd ever witnessed before. Part decay, part death, and part dirt it was. I had to wash myself good when I got home.

It wasn't long before Man-Jack and Toomy weren't going home with me at night anymore, but were staying with the other workers.

You could see the prison changing, every day. We labored, cleaning, burning refuse, raking and sweeping, pulling weeds, digging, hammering. The wagon came from Macon from General Wilson, with supplies. There was plenty of food now, and we had to put the crates in the creek to keep the food fresh.

Finally, one day in June Mr. Griffin asked: "You want to go into the cemetery now, Eulinda?"

I'd almost forgotten about Neddy's ring. And truth to

tell, it wasn't on my mind as Mr. Griffin and I made our way up the dirt road to where the men were now working.

Inside the not-yet-completed fence we stood in silence, Mr. Griffin and I. And the silence of the place pounded in my ears, in my blood, in my bones.

The silence was like a battery of cannon, assaulting my senses. Here were thousands upon thousands of markers, some just crude sticks stuck in formation in the earth.

"They've been buried in trenches," Mr. Griffin said softly. "As far as I can figure out, there are a hundred to a hundred and fifty in each trench."

My heart fell. In trenches! Then it lifted. They wouldn't bury the colored troops with the others. "Do you know where the colored graves are?" I asked.

"No, Eulinda. I haven't any records. General Wilson said his men took them to Washington. Our only hope is that the bodies were marked. We begin work soon on reburying."

I nodded silently.

"It's all I can do," he said. "I'm sorry."

No white person had ever told me they were sorry about anything in my life.

"You don't have to stay, if you don't want, Eulinda. I know the work is hard. You cook as well as help us. You may go home if you wish."

"I'll stay," I said. But I went home that night with my spirit cast down. I might never find Neddy! Mistis scolded, because the chicken didn't have the right flavor and the biscuits were overdone, because Man-Jack and Toomy weren't coming home anymore. She blamed me for that. Mr. Hampton was in his study, recovering from another of his spells.

"Really, Eulinda, I'm going to have to hire a cook. I cannot survive on such food."

"If the prisoners had had such food, they'd have lived."

Her fork clattered on the plate. "If you insist on speaking of that dreadful place, I shall forbid you to go anymore."

"I'm free," I told her. "You can't forbid me."

"My husband can. You are his daughter."

"Then why doesn't he do something for me?"

"What do you want us to do, Eulinda?"

"Send me North. So I can go to school."

"We do not wish to lose you, dear," she said icily.

Indeed, I was underage. I was trapped. I cried myself to sleep that night with bitter tears of helplessness.

And then the next morning, still feeling heavy of spirit, when I trudged to report to Mr. Griffin at his desk under the tent, he smiled at me. "You look like the last wagon in a bad-luck supply train. What's wrong?"

"Nothing, sir."

"Well, I have good news! Received word after you left yesterday. We're getting help, lots of it. Clara Barton is coming from Washington, with a fellow named Dorence Atwater. He was a prisoner here. And he has lists of the dead."

"You look so happy, Mr. Griffin. Like a whole army is coming to help. Who is Clara Barton?" I asked.

"A whole army," he said.

CHAPTER TWELVE

How I Went to Work
for the Most Powerful Woman
in the World

IT WAS SO HOT THE DAY WE WAITED FOR Clara Barton that you could see the heat shimmering over the land.

Mr. Griffin said she was coming with white cavalry. And Negro troops. I supposed her to be like one of those princesses in the books Annalee used to read, with a tall, pointed hat and a gauzy veil and a horse with a bridle of gold.

I stood with Mr. Griffin, waiting to greet her. Below, outside the gates of the prison, were at least twenty local Negroes, waiting, too.

"What do they want?" Mr. Griffin asked me.

"I suppose they found out about the Negro troops, sir, and wanted to see them."

"Tell me, who is this gentleman approaching us, Eulinda?"

"It's Mr. Porter from Poplar Hill, sir. He won't be happy about the Negro troops."

He wasn't. "We don't want Negro troops around here," he told Mr. Griffin. "It might incite those freedmen against us more than they are already."

Mr. Griffin nodded. "I assure you, there is nothing to worry about. It's General Wilson's wish, and he is the ranking Federal official in the area."

"Ranking Federal official be damned," Porter said. "The Yankees will soon be sorry they gave Negroes guns."

Then he took note of me. "You're Mrs. Kellogg's Negro girl, aren't you?"

No more, I wanted to say, but I didn't. "Yessir."

"What are you doing here?"

"She's working for me. For pay," Mr. Griffin said.

Mr. Porter gave Mr. Griffin a look of contempt. Then he said to me, "Don't you get any fancy notions when you see those Negro troops. We whites are still in charge." And he turned on his heel and left.

❧ • ❧

Clara Barton did not wear a pointed hat or a gauzy veil. She was plain as a field mouse in her dark gray dress with the white collar and her hair all bundled up behind her head.

She came with forty workmen and clerks and all kinds of supplies, wood for white headboards, ink for black lettering, and Dorence Atwater, the man with the death rolls.

"This is Mr. Atwater," she told us. And the tall young man with the broad shoulders and hundred-year-old eyes gave a little bow. "He has lists of the dead, so we can identify their graves, and let their loved ones know where they rest."

Clara Barton isn't the princess, I thought, she's the fairy godmother with the magic wand.

After her workmen finished putting up her tent, I stood outside it with a tray of tea. I'd made biscuits. I was no longer to do the cooking. The Negro cook was better at it than I.

My new duties, Mr. Griffin had said, were to be a help-mate to Clara Barton. If she wanted me.

Before I announced myself, I watched her for a moment. She was setting out her writing materials on a small camp desk. Late afternoon sun made the inside of the tent full of yellow light. Mr. Griffin had said she was one of the most famous women in the world. And she got famous by helping others.

"How did she help them?" I asked.

"Why don't you ask her," was all he'd answered.

So I aimed to. Soon's I got the back roads of my tongue unstuck. Then I saw her struggling with the buttons in back of her dress. "Miss Barton? I can help you with that."

She turned and smiled. "Ah, you are the girl Mr. Griffin told me about. I certainly can use help, thank you."

I helped her with the buttons and reached for her silk robe on the bed. But she held out a hand to stop me.

"You are not my maid, child. But you can be my secretary if you wish. Mr. Griffin told me you are educated."

I loved her for that, right off. She poured her own tea. Then she asked me to tell her about myself. I did so, slowly at first, but soon I was telling about Neddy being buried in the cemetery (though I didn't mention the ring), about Mistis, and about how she had threatened me.

"Has Mr. Kellogg offered to take you into the house as his daughter?" she asked. "Or provide for your future?"

"No," I said. "He goes everyday more inside his head. Times it feels like he doesn't even know who I am. It's because his son is missing in the war."

"Perhaps I can help find his son."

"Oh, ma'am, that would be wonderful!"

"It would take time, of course. And first, I would say that if he has never acknowledged you, legally, as his daughter, then he has no rights to hold you. Do you want to leave?"

I shrugged. "Where would I go?"

She smiled. "Why not right here? With me. It's a big tent. I could use the company in the midst of all these men. Captain Moore, the head of all the troops, does not like me. He cannot abide women anywhere in the public arena. And he wants credit for my idea of coming here to restore this place."

"But Mr. Griffin said you are one of the most powerful women in the world."

"And that is why Captain Moore does not like me. My dear, sometimes I feel very alone. If you want to leave your people and come and work for me, I would be most delighted."

Something there was, right away, between me and this woman. Some connection. Some electricity, as Mr. Hampton would put it. I felt it, and I'm sure she did, too. "Yes, ma'am," I said. "I'd like that very much."

My head was swirling. Here was a woman who got things done. Then I turned at the tent flap. "Miss Barton, how did you become famous all over the world?"

She sighed. "It was very simple. The important men in Washington started a war with no thought in mind of caring for their wounded. So I had to do it," she said.

"How?"

"I set up field hospitals. I started campaigns with my friends in the North to send food, supplies, money. Why, they had no hospitals when I started, child. I set wounded men up in the hallways of public buildings!"

A woman did all this, I thought.

"I worked all through the war," she said softly. "I attended meetings of Congress and the Supreme Court. I learned who to see for favors. And I had to overcome the idea men have that women are weak and useless."

Her smile was tender. "And then, my brother, who had joined the Confederate army, wrote that he was being held in a Union prison. Because I was superintendent of nurses for the Army of the James, I could get him out. But he was so sickly! I tried to nurse him back to health. But he died. And then people started writing to me about their loved ones who had marched off to war and never been heard of again. There are so many."

I left with my veins throbbing with excitement. So. Those important men in Washington gave no nevermind to how they were going to care for soldiers who got shot in the war, and she did. It was simple, she said.

I felt a world opening up before me as I trudged home that evening to make supper.

By the time I got home my mind was set. I would leave Pond Bluff. I would tell them tonight.

CHAPTER THIRTEEN

How I Left Pond Bluff and Said Good-bye to Mr. Hampton

"MR. HAMPTON, SIR, MAY I HAVE A WORD with you?"

I tried to stand straight, and speak soft and plain like Miss Barton. But my knees were shaking.

It was after supper. I'd cleaned up the dishes and taken a long look around the dining room, and I felt fear and a pang of sadness.

I was going to leave this. And for what? A tent at the prison? Well, I thought, chuckling to myself, Well, Moll always did say I was a little bit crazy.

"Mr. Hampton, sir?"

He sat at his desk, on which there were an assortment of papers, vials of powder and liquid.

"Hey? Eulinda? Come in, child."

I went in, keeping my eyes away from the tall-case clock, the book lined walls, the secretary in the corner, the bowl of flowers on the table in the middle of the Persian carpet. All these things had hands now, which were reaching out to me, voices that were saying *Stay, Eulinda, stay.*

"Mr. Hampton, I'm leaving."

I had yet to pack my things, but I had few things to pack. An old rag doll I'd played with as a child, some books, one change of clothing. And, of course, my dog.

"Leaving? It's late to go to town, isn't it?"

"Not to town, sir."

"Oh, the prison. You have an errand there tonight?"

"No, Mr. Hampton, I mean I'm leaving for good. I won't be back anymore, sir. I'm going away."

Now he put down his papers and looked at me. When had he gotten so old, I wondered? When had his hair turned white? "Mr. Hampton, I wanted to tell you, so's you'd know."

I held my breath, waiting. The tall-case clock ticked. My blood pounded in my ears. Would he forbid it? Would he make a claim on me? Would he offer me something to stay? And if he did, would I have the mettle to say no?

"For good? I don't understand those words, Eulinda."

"They mean I won't be back. Ever. I'm going to be living in a tent at the prison for the next month. With Miss Clara Barton, who's come to help. She's a very important woman and she's asked me to be her secretary and helpmate."

"I know who Clara Barton is."

He was having a lucid moment. Good. I thought to tell him she was going to try to find Mr. Julian. But then I decided no, I don't want to make him any promises I can't keep. He's done that to me, but I won't do that to him.

"But you cannot leave us, Eulinda. Why would you do such a thing? Why you've always lived here. Haven't we been good to you, child?"

"Yes, Mr. Hampton, you have. And I appreciate everything you have done for me. Teaching me, I mean. But the war is over now and I'm free, and I have to start thinking about making my own way. Like Sancho and Moll and the others. And there isn't anything for me here, sir. So I'm going."

I'd rehearsed my speech while I was making supper. I'd told myself to be calm, not to cry, and to be firm with him.

"There's so much we want to do for you, child." He shook his head. "You're family."

"No sir, I'm not family. I mean, when you decide I am, I am, but then Mistis gets angry about something and she decides I'm not. I can't live like that, Mr. Hampton. I have to be one thing or the other. And I've thought on it and decided I'd rather make my own way."

I saw his bewilderment, his hurt, and I felt sad. Then I remembered Miss Barton's words. That he had never acknowledged me, legally, as his daughter. And I thought, too, And he's not defended me against Mistis. It had made no nevermind to him when I went to live in the slave cabin.

"Very well, then, Eulinda," he said. "If you must go, go."

I stood stock-still. Was that all? He wasn't going to insist that I stay? He wasn't going to come to me and put his arms around me and call me "daughter"?

Through the tears in my eyes, I saw him go back to his papers. He no longer paid any mind to me.

He wasn't going to say "Go with God?" Or wish me luck?

I shifted my weight from one foot to the other. The moments were strung out like popcorn on a string for the Christmas tree. And I knew that if I didn't soon leave, the string would break, and I'd break and fall into pieces like popcorn, all over the floor.

"Good-bye, Mr. Hampton," I said.

But he did not hear me as I left the room.

CHAPTER FOURTEEN

Dorence Atwater Tells Me His Tale

"BY SEPTEMBER OF SIXTY-FOUR, I WAS WRITING one hundred names a day on my death rolls," Dorence Atwater told me. "And watching them cart off the naked skeletons of my comrades in the death carts every day."

We were sitting at a table under the trees a bit away from the stockade. Captain Moore and some men sat at a distance, some painting the white headboards, some lettering them with the name, unit, and day of death in black letters. Other men were digging up bodies from the shallow trenches in the cemetery and burying them in separate graves.

It was a week since I'd left Pond Bluff. Mr. Atwater's death rolls had told exactly who was buried where in the cemetery. He could tell where Neddy was buried. He was going to take me, today, to Neddy's grave.

But first he seemed to want to talk. We were finishing our breakfast coffee. We ate every morning together, he and Miss Barton and I. She had left the table to make custard and black tea for one of the other clerks, who was down with a malignant fever.

Captain Moore had put the sick clerk in the same tent as Mr. Atwater, and Miss Barton was worried for Atwater. "Captain Moore does it to get back at me," she'd said. But Mr. Atwater didn't seem to mind. He'd been through worse in the war, he'd told her.

And now he was set on telling me.

"How did you keep your death rolls away from the prison authorities?" I asked. I was taken with him. He had seen so much. He was a walking record of this place. He may even have seen my brother. Yet he had survived.

I had to know how. I sensed there was something I could learn from him. And I had to trust him. I knew that already, because I knew he'd want to bury Neddy proper-like. He considered that part of his job around here, if he had to disturb a grave. So I knew I must tell him about the ring.

"I hid my death rolls from the authorities," he said. "You see, I was a store clerk before the war. I came here in February of sixty-four, after being captured at Gettysburg. I spent five months in Belle Isle prison in Richmond, starving and freezing and sickly, before I came here."

Dorence Atwater had a twitch in his face, and I could see that talking about his imprisonment brought it on. "After I was here a while they asked me to be a clerk in the prison hospital. I was to keep a record of all the prisoners in the hospital. I was to record the names, units, and dates of those who died, cause of death and grave number. They said the list would be turned over to Union officials at the end of the war. But I did not believe them, so I kept another list. I hid my list inside my shirt or pants whenever an officer came into the office. When I returned into the stockade at night, I'd transfer the names on my list to my ledger book. Then I'd wrap my ledger in waterproof cloth and hide it in my shebang. They never found it."

He stopped for a moment, looking down at his hands, then went on. "Then I'd go to the cemetery when the dead were buried and record the name and grave number of each dead prisoner. The bodies were supposed to have tags on them. But sometimes they lay in the dead house too long, and the tags would be gone. I'd run around trying to find out who the dead fellow was before he was buried. I had to be back in the stockade before dark. I worked late many nights in the office, keeping the death rolls. If I was late the sentries would fire at me if I was outside the stockade after dusk."

"And you made a map of the cemetery, too," I said.

"Yes."

"And Miss Barton said you were sick, too."

He shrugged. "Everyone was. Last winter it was cold, damp, and muddy. I had fevers all the time. And pneumonia. And because I worked in the hospital I could get better food. Then last February they moved me out. To a prison in North Carolina. I spent two days there, then was sent to Union lines. By then I was weak. I had malnutrition. I still had fevers. I still had my lists. I went home to my family in Connecticut. And then I got a telegram from the Secretary of War, Stanton. He wanted me to turn over my lists. So I did a stupid thing, and did so."

"And?" I asked.

"I got there the afternoon of the day President Lincoln was shot. I handed my lists over to the War Department. Next morning the city was in chaos. Stanton was half-mad, trying to catch the assassins. They thanked me for my lists and offered me three hundred dollars for them. I didn't want the money. I wanted to be assured my lists would be published in the papers. But other lists of dead from other prisons had already been published and the public was in outrage over all the dead. Stanton said that to publish the list of thirteen thousand dead prisoners from Andersonville would not be good for the country's morale."

"Thirteen thousand?" I asked.

"Yes. Thirteen thousand. All those families wondering where their sons, brothers, and husbands were. And not knowing."

He fell silent for a moment, then went on. "I fought with the War Department. They told me they'd return my lists, as soon as they could be copied and said they'd pay off my father's medical bills if I stopped making trouble. Well, my father was very sick and soon died. I started writing to influential people to get my lists back. One of them was Clara Barton. That's all I can say of the matter now."

I stood up. "Miss Barton says your lists made it possible to find every body in the cemetery."

He looked across the table at me. "Yes," he said. "And so, are you ready to see your brother's grave?"

"Yes, Mr. Atwater. Only first, I must tell you something."

CHAPTER FIFTEEN

We Find and Rebury Neddy and Thomas Jefferson's Grandson, and I Find What I Came For, But Am No Longer Sure I Want It

I TOLD HIM ABOUT THE RING AS HE GRABBED up a shovel and we put on our gloves and walked up the dirt road to the cemetery.

"And you think he has it on him?" Atwater asked.

"I don't know. But I need help finding it. I hate to ask you, Mr. Atwater, but could you help me?"

"Of course. When did you say he came here?"

"I think it was February of last year."

He sighed and looked around. We were in the cemetery. Some parts of it were being dug up by Captain Moore's men. In other parts, neat white headboards already rose in the Georgia earth.

"That's a long spell to be here," he said, "and Negro

troops weren't treated well at all. They had a white commander who was wounded. His name was Boyle, I think. Yes, Archibald Boyle. When he got here he was near death from his wounds. The doctor refused to treat him. The Negro soldiers did, with makeshift remedies."

"Did he live?"

"Yes. And Miss Barton tells me he is going to testify at the trial of Henry Wirz, which begins next month. But he was always sickly when he was here, always sneaking into the hospital for treatment and being thrown out. Just because he commanded Negro troops."

He looked at me. "All the prisoners had to sell whatever valuables they had, just to get food to stay alive. So the ring may not be with your brother's remains, Eulinda. But if it is, I will find it for you."

With that promised, he set about, pulling out a map of the cemetery, mumbling to himself for a while.

"It was stolen from the first Mrs. Kellogg by my brother Neddy," I told him. "I don't want you to make yourself part of anything unsavory, Mr. Atwater."

He gave a short laugh. "Can anything be more unsavory than all this?" He gestured around him. "That ring belongs to you, Eulinda. Your little brother was sold away because of it. Now let's see, it says here that Thomas Eston Hemings is buried in this plot right here."

He rested his hand on a splintery cross.

"Oh," I said. "Neddy wrote of him to me. He was the grandson of Thomas Jefferson."

"So I have been led to believe. So he was a friend of your brother's. Then Neddy should be buried in one of these graves right here. You see, because there weren't so many colored troops, Eulinda, they weren't buried in common trenches like the white men. In a way, you coloreds are more fortunate."

"I'm sorry that Mr. Jefferson's grandson didn't make it out," I told him.

He hushed me, concentrating. In a short time he found Neddy's grave. He started digging. The red clay earth was dusty and loose and yielded to his shovel. As he dug, he talked.

"The authorities here were terrified of the Negro prisoners of war."

"Why?"

"Everyone in the South was terrified of seeing a Negro man in a uniform, toting a gun. It was their nightmare come true. They feared the sight of the colored soldiers would incite the slaves to rebellion."

I thought about Neddy. He was always angry, but the thought of him inciting anything made me smile.

"There were only about a hundred Negro soldiers

here, to my recollection," he went on. "They kept to themselves. They had a little territory staked out by the south gate. They were made to do hard labor. They dug earthwork defenses. That's when they were flogged, when they resisted that labor."

"Did many resist?" I asked.

"A lot," he said.

And I knew then that Neddy would have resisted. Anything that made him appear like a slave he would resist, to the death.

≈ • ≈

When he reached a certain depth in the ground, Dorence Atwater bade me stand back. I obeyed.

He set down his shovel and masked his face, then knelt down on the ground. What was he doing?

"Mr. Atwater?" I asked. I knelt beside him. He raised his right arm to keep me back so's I couldn't see into the grave.

"Remember your brother as he was when he was alive," he said.

For a few moments we knelt together. Then he went about doing more of whatever he was doing in the grave, and when he turned to me he handed me the ring.

I could not believe it! Neddy's ring! He hadn't sold it for food. He'd kept it, perhaps even died because of lack of food, but he'd kept the ring Zeke had been sold away for!

It was dirt encrusted and had to be cleaned, but there was the ruby stone and the gold band, same as ever.

Dorence Atwater took the tag from Neddy's body and gave that to me, too. The writing was blurred, but it said that Neddy had died on the seventeenth of November, Year of Our Lord 1864.

I tried to recollect what I was doing around that time, but couldn't. I couldn't think at all, matter of fact.

"I'm sorry," Dorence Atwater said to me.

"Mr. Atwater, you have no need to be sorry."

"We all do," he said.

"I waited then under a nearby tree while he covered over Neddy's bones proper like, and marked the splinter cross with the tag. Then he did the same for the grave of Thomas Jefferson's grandson. When he finished, we left. I thought how there was something fitting about Neddy's lying next to Jefferson's grandson. But I could not think then what the something fitting was.

"I don't know if I can keep this ring," I told him on the way down the hill. "It doesn't seem right, taking it from a place like this and using it for my own ends."

"You give yourself a while to think on it," he said.

CHAPTER SIXTEEN

How I Started Painting Grave Markers, and How the Caters Came to Us

ON THE WAY BACK FROM THE CEMETERY I asked Mr. Atwater if I could letter the wooden sign for Neddy's grave.

"You have to ask Captain Moore," he said. "He's in charge of that detail."

"Captain? Sir?" I stood a bit away from the table where he sat painting with three of his men.

He looked up. He had a full beard, and his eyes were hard. I felt those eyes go over me, from head to toe. "Yes?"

"I'd like to paint the headboard for my brother's grave."

"You have a brother here?"

"Yessir. Mr. Atwater found him for me. I do good lettering."

"You're the girl who helps Miss Barton. You're educated, I hear."

"Yessir."

He grunted. "All right. Private?" He spoke to one of his men. "Give her a headboard. "If you do well Miss—what's your name?"

"Eulinda, sir."

"If you do well, you can help us with some other headboards. We've got about three hundred done. We have to do thirteen thousand."

"Yessir." It seemed that I had gotten myself into a fine kettle of fish here. I took my tools and went off a bit to sit under a tree with Otis beside me. I spent most of that afternoon writing Neddy's name, rank, regiment, and date of death on the headboard. Captain Moore and his men had removed themselves to another task, and I was the only one visible outside the gates of the stockade.

I looked up from my painstaking work to see a tall man who could only be described as a mulatto, coming across the grass toward me. "Could you direct me to Miss Barton?"

He was middling well dressed and very handsome. "I believe she's caring for one of our sick helpers," I said.

"Please do sit." I gestured to a chair. "Can I help you in any way?"

"You work with her?"

I told him about myself, to gain his trust. He sat with his hat in his hands and began hesitantly.

"My name is Arnold Cater. I was a house slave for William Rabon, governor of Georgia," he said quietly. "I was married to a good woman, but the Rabons sold me to help pay for their daughter's wedding. I was sent to southwestern Georgia, some two hundred miles away. My new master's name was Nick Wylie. I knew I'd never see my wife and children again, so I took myself another wife, a slave of Wylie's. We had a child. Early this year my wife was expecting another child and supposed to be doing a harsh task. But she couldn't do it well enough for the overseer, so he whipped her on her back 'til the blood flowed. That's the way I found her. She couldn't even stand. Then that overseer said if she didn't finish the work by morning, he'd be back and beat her more. So we ran off. Left our baby."

A sob escaped his throat. "We come to Americus. Some Negro friends took us in and found me work as a blacksmith. Then the war ended and I heard tell of this Miss Clara Barton up here. I hear such good things about her. And I've come to ask her. Should I go back to the

Wylie plantation now that the war's over? Should I go back and get our baby? And, could we live here? Would we be safe? I left my wife in Americus."

I put down the headboard and my paints and brush and stood up. "You wait right here, Mr. Cater," I told him. "I'll fetch Miss Barton."

꧁ · ꧂

That very afternoon, with Miss Barton telling me the words, I sat at the same table with her and Mr. Cater and wrote a letter to the Union commander at Americus.

"I ask you to dispatch a sergeant and a wagon this day," I wrote in my best handwriting, "to fetch the Cater baby, their bedroom furniture, and their chickens and send them on to Americus where Mr. Cater would be waiting."

I never saw anyone so grateful as Mr. Cater. He thanked us profusely. There were tears in his eyes when he left.

I watched him go. "He lost his five children and his first wife when he was sold away," I told Miss Barton.

"It's a familiar story," she said.

Two days later an old, dilapidated wagon pulled up in front of the south gate. In it were Mr. Cater, his wife and baby, their meager bedroom furniture, and three crates of chickens.

"Miss Barton, Miss Barton!" Mr. Cater shouted as he ran across the grass at us. "This here's my wife, Lily, and our baby! That letter worked like a charm! How can I help you? I'll help out here in any way I can, and my wife, too. If you just give us a little corner to live in."

Lily was as light-skinned as her husband, with a round, sweet face and a pleasant manner. And she was very heavy with child. The baby in her arms was about a year and a half old, and fussing. I took it from her. Miss Barton led her to a chair under a tree and poured her some lemonade.

We had a helping woman about the place now, by the name of Rosa. She was a Negro. She worked as nurse and washerwoman. Her husband, Jarret, took care of the soldiers' horses, and could do carpentry. They had come to us two weeks before, lost and wandering, just like the Caters.

Rosa knew a lot about babies. She took the Cater baby from me and walked it around under the trees. She sent her husband for something for it to sleep in. He brought an old dresser drawer. "I'll make a little cradle tonight," he promised.

"Miss Barton," I heard Mr. Cater begging softly, "you got to let us stay. My wife can cook. I'm a good blacksmith. We got no place else to go, and my wife is too close to her time to travel back to Americus."

Miss Barton secured a tent for them, which she had the men set not far from the one she and I occupied.

They stayed. Mr. Cater was engaged as a blacksmith. His wife did light chores. I went on with my headboard painting.

Captain Moore had approved of my lettering job and set me to doing other headboards. I found that if I worked diligently I could do three a day and still have time to help Miss Barton. And even play with Otis a bit.

I scarce thought of Pond Bluff at all.

⁂

In the next week the white headboards bloomed in the earth like flowers. On moonlit nights you could see them up there in the cemetery, a whiteness against the surrounding dark, like the lost souls whose places they marked forever.

In daytime the vast graveyard now was neat and orderly. Miss Barton had brought some flower seeds and planted them about. They would bloom, in full, next summer, when none of us would be here, when we would all be gone our separate ways.

Under the hot summer sun we settled into a set pattern. Not a day went by that I didn't write a letter, with Miss Barton saying the words, to help someone who was working for us. We wrote letters seeking lost relatives almost daily. Every one of the workers had someone missing, it seemed.

Miss Barton even wrote a letter to Elmira Prison, asking after Mr. Julian.

Rosa and Lily were both cooking now, as well as one of Captain Moore's men. When we took our meals we sat at tables under the trees, with Captain Moore's men broken up at different sections, and Dorence Atwater, myself, and Miss Barton at our own camp. Lily took her meals with us. Mr. Griffin wandered at leisure, speaking to everyone. The Negro troops and workers set themselves apart and there was a great deal of laughter and talk from them. Toomy and Man-Jack stayed with them.

The Negro freedmen who'd come to help from the neighborhood could not lay by their awe at the Negro troops, and never ceased to ask about their exploits in the war.

One day, after Lily had left the table to see to her baby, Miss Barton said, "I'd like to take them back to Washington with me. But my money for this expedition is just about spent. I've even used some of my own funds."

The she paused before continuing. "I would so like to do something for the living who have been so harmed by this war, as well as for the dead."

Neither Dorence nor I said anything.

"I'd like to take you, too, Eulinda. Would you like to come with me to Washington and continue as my secretary? We must think of the future now that this project is nearly finished. What say you?"

All I could do was get up, go round to her and hug her, by way of an answer.

CHAPTER SEVENTEEN

How We Help Even More People, and I Am Given a Sign

NEXT AFTERNOON A DELEGATION OF NEGROES came to the front of the south gate and asked for admission.

Mr. Griffin brought them to where I was still painting my headboards. My hands and apron were covered with black paint. I had a headache from painting all morning and my hair was askew. I looked like something Otis had worried to the bone.

"Miss Eulinda," Mr. Griffin said, "these people have heard that Miss Barton can help them. Would you fetch her, please?"

I looked into the many black faces who were staring at me. Some of the heads were gray, one or two women held children in their arms. The men wore ragged breeches and their faces all glistened with a sheen of sweat.

The whole world needs help, I thought, as I ran to fetch Miss Barton. And half of it has come to us.

Miss Barton was in Dorence Atwater's tent, caring for Edward Watts, who was still sick. I'd forgotten that the doctor had come that morning to visit him.

"Don't come in!" he shouted, as I called for Miss Barton. So I waited outside the tent. When she came out, wiping her hands dry, she shook her head.

"I'm afraid Mr. Watts has typhoid," she said. "Dr. Bledsoe has given him Dover's powders and some quinine. I can't get Dorence to move out of the tent, and I fear for his health. Perhaps you can influence him, Eulinda."

I said I would try. "There are a lot of Negro people here to see you, Miss Barton," I said.

She sighed, and gathered her skirts to walk down the hill and meet the Negroes.

✺ • ✺

"Miss Clara, Miss Clara," they called out as we came near. And I heard some say. "Here she come. The Yankee woman."

As we approached the table I saw there were gifts laid there. Baskets of peaches, chickens, tomatoes.

There were grinning faces and outstretched hands as she went amongst them. "I ain't never seen a Yankee woman before," one Negro woman whose head was wrapped in a gaily colored turban said. "My, ain't you grand!"

"I'm afraid I'm not so grand at the moment," she told them. "I've been working hard all morning, planting flowers in the cemetery and nursing one of our helpers who is down sick."

"You do fer others. That's what make you grand," the same Negro woman said.

She shook every hand. She patted the babies. She invited them to sit on the grass under the shade of the tree and I helped Rosa pour them lemonade. She bade Lily to fetch a loaf or two of fresh bread from the bake house. I helped slice it up and soon they were all eating.

One old gray-headed man stood up. "The reason why we come, Miss Clara, 'sides to meet you, is to ask, is Mr. Lincoln really dead, like we been tol'?"

"Yes," she answered.

"White folks where we all comes from said that if'n he be dead we be slaves agin. We be thinkin' he not dead and white folks tellin' us this as a hoax, to get us to be slaves agin. If you tell us he dead, but we still free, we believe it."

Miss Barton looked into a sea of at least twenty-five faces. "Mr. Lincoln is dead," she told them quietly. "It was a terrible tragedy. He was shot. I saw him dead. But you are still free. You will always be free, and don't believe anyone who tells you otherwise."

There were some murmured *glories* and *amens.*

"Besides," she continued, "before he died, he signed the Emancipation Proclamation, which is a paper making you free."

The same elderly black man spoke again. "We heard that if we worked the fields for our old white masters we were supposed to git some of the crops. But when we tol' 'em this, they run us off, Miss Clara. What should we do?"

She told them. "I shall get both a copy of the Emancipation and a copy of the order written by General Wilson, the Union commander in this area. I shall read both to you all. Come back at the end of the week."

"But we gots no place to go, until then, Miss Clara," the elderly Negro said. "We been run off by our old white masters."

Miss Barton thought for a moment. "If you all will help the Negroes who are working here, I shall see to it that you are provided with both shelter and food. But when I get the proper papers, you must go back to your planta- tions. Is it agreed?"

It was agreed. And so that afternoon I took a trip into Andersonville with Miss Barton, to get the proper papers.

⚜ • ⚜

Just as we were about to go into the provost marshal's office in town, a woman called out to us.

"Miss Barton, is that you?"

It was Mistis herself, yelling to get our attention like she was calling home the hogs. With her was a Negro woman I did not know, a young woman who carried her basket. "Why, Eulinda," Mistis exclaimed, seeing me. "How are you, dear?"

"I'm fine, ma'am."

"I am so sorry we didn't get to say a proper good-bye." She turned her attention to Miss Barton. "I am Mrs. Hampton Kellogg of Pond Bluff. Eulinda was my protégé, you know. I taught her to read and write. Why ever she wanted to go to that terrible place and help clean up a graveyard is beyond me."

"I suppose it would be," Miss Barton said.

Her sarcasm was lost on Mistis. "I know I am late with this invitation, and I am so ashamed no one in the area extended one before this. But you must come to tea at Pond Bluff. We have all heard about the wonderful work you are doing at the prison. You will come, won't you?"

Miss Barton said yes.

"How about Wednesday afternoon? Can you see your way clear? Or must you check with your secretary?"

"My secretary is right here." Miss Barton turned to me. "Eulinda, are we free on Wednesday afternoon?"

I shall always love Miss Clara Barton for that. "Yes, ma'am," I said. "I think we can spare the time."

I saw Mistis's eyes go wide with surprise. "I shall have some ladies from the area so you can meet them. I must hurry home and write the invitations. You see," and she gave a gay little laugh, "I don't have a secretary."

Then, as we were about to part, she stopped. "Oh, Eulinda, I forgot to ask. Did you find any trace of Neddy?"

I felt myself quicken with fear. "We found his grave," I said.

"Oh, dear Neddy, he meant so much to my husband. Was he buried properly? I understand that is the purpose of the good people working now at the prison."

"Yes, ma'am," I said. "I was there. He was."

"Well, I hate to push an indelicate subject, but did you, or, any other person, happen to find a ring in his grave?"

I just stared at her. My mouth went dry. Blood pounded in my ears. "No," I said.

She turned then to Miss Barton. "The ring belonged to my husband's first wife. His mind isn't the same since his son went missing. If it is returned to him, the sentimental value will ease his soul. Neddy had it when he went off to war. The details are foggy in my mind, how he got it, but that doesn't matter now. All that matters is that it should be returned to my husband."

"I'll ask about," Miss Barton said. "Any valuables found on the dead are turned in."

I stumbled through my errands with Miss Barton that morning. If she sensed I was distracted, she did not say. Nor did she ask me about the ring. All she did say was, "That woman is a viper. How could you have worked for her?"

"I had no choice," I said.

What should I do? Tell Miss Barton about the ring? I must tell her, I decided. But it must be the right moment. A thought was forming in my mind about that ring, which I kept in a tied handkerchief in my apron pocket. A thought I could not get a good purchase on yet.

But when we got home that afternoon with the proper papers in hand, Arnold Cater came rushing to meet us. "Oh, Miss Barton, come quick! My Lily's time has come. Rosa is with her, but she is asking for you!"

I watched Miss Barton go to the Cater tent. I offered to watch the baby. I set her down on the ground next to me on a quilt as I finished a headboard I'd started that morning.

From the Cater tent I heard Lily's cries of distress. I continued painting the headboard and watching the Cater baby. The hot sun beat overhead, the baby cried, and I took her into our tent and gave her some water and tried to rock her to sleep. But she was fussing, so I lay down on the cot next to her, and to the drone of insects outside, the faraway talk of some workmen, and Lily's occasional cries, I fell asleep, with Otis at my feet.

~· ~

It was Arnold Cater who woke me. "Miss Eulinda?"

I sat up. Sweat made the back of my blouse cling to me, and for a moment I could not think where I was. Arnold Cater had picked up his baby and stood in front of me, smiling.

"We got a new little baby, Miss Eulinda. His name is Zeke."

"Oh, I'm so happy. How is Lily?"

"Sitting up, perkier than a woman who just gave birth has a right to be. Think of it, Miss Eulinda! A baby born. In this terrible place. A birth!"

It came to me then what he had said earlier. "Zeke?" I asked. "You named the baby Zeke?"

"Why yes, Miss Eulinda. I thought my Lily told you. I had three girls and a boy when I was sold away. The boy's name was Zeke. We've named this little boy after him. Why? Is something wrong?"

I thought of the wonder of it, how he and Lily had come here, to this dolorous corner of the earth for help. And I had come to be here working, and then Lily had this baby and named him after my brother who was sold away. Without even knowing the story. How can this be, I asked myself? How?

"No," I told him. "Everything is wonderful, Arnold, wonderful." And then, just roused from sleep by that good man who had suffered so, still in the grip of dreams, I got a purchase on the thought in my head about the ring. It's a sign, I told myself. I've been given a sign. And I knew what I was going to do.

∽◦ · ◦∾

The next morning Miss Barton and I awoke to find the twenty-five Negroes who had come to her for help waiting outside her tent.

We dressed quickly. "Hand me the papers," she said. "And stand beside me."

I did so. I could see she was scarce awake, but she got the papers in order quickly, then, in the mists of morning, she read Mr. Lincoln's proclamation.

There was a chorus of amens. Some of the men stood with their hats over their hearts. All of the people had bowed heads.

"Now I wish to tell you," Miss Barton said, "that according to these orders written by General Wilson, he advises you to remain on the estates of your former masters until Christmas, to gather in the crops you planted and await further arrangements by the Federal government. Also in these papers he orders the whites to give you a share of the crops as wages if they do not have the proper currency. Under no conditions are you to work for nothing, and if you have any further trouble, go to the provost marshal's office in Andersonville."

There was a great deal of jubilation. The Negroes crowded around, thanking Miss Barton. By the afternoon of that day, they were gone back to their old plantations.

CHAPTER EIGHTEEN

How I Take Tea at Pond Bluff, and Mistis Is Put in Her Place at Long Last

YOU DON'T IGNORE A SIGN WHEN IT IS GIVEN to you. That's what Mama always said. I wasn't ignoring it, though. I just didn't have time to do yet what I knew I should do.

Miss Barton was busy caring for Mr. Watts, who was getting worse and worse. I did talk to Mr. Atwater and convince him to move to another tent.

"If you get sick," I told him, "Miss Barton will blame herself." So he moved for Miss Barton.

By Wednesday noon I was working on headboards that said UNKNOWN U.S. SOLDIER.

There were to be four hundred and fifty-one of them, according to Mr. Atwater's death rolls. I was just completing my fifth one when Miss Barton told me to dress. It was time for tea at Pond Bluff.

❧ · ☙

I wanted to tell her right off about the ring as we started on our way in the wagon. But she started talking about herself, and truth to tell, I was so interested, I didn't interrupt.

"I've never married, Eulinda. Though I have had many proposals," she said. "I know there is talk about me. And speculation. I just wanted to tell you that."

"Yes, ma'am."

"I never liked the restrictions placed on married women. I have my father's warrior blood in my veins. He was a soldier who served with General Mad Anthony Wayne in the Michigan Territory. My older brothers taught me to ride and shoot. Did you know I can hit the bull's-eye of a target at fifty feet?"

I said no, I didn't.

"I have a great love of family. You should know about me, since you're leaving your home and coming with me to Washington City. When brother Stephen died, I turned to my true work, finding missing soldiers from the war. By that time there was a prisoner exchange and I went, with Mr. Lincoln's blessing, to Annapolis, Maryland, where men from the Southern prisons were being sent, to find missing soldiers."

I listened to her talk about her brothers, her father, her nephews. She had sent a young girl to music school in Boston. She'd cared for her brother David through an illness when she was only thirteen.

"I was the last child. Sister Sally was eleven years older than I, Stephen fifteen, David thirteen, and Dorothy seventeen. They raised me. My parents had a very troubled marriage."

"I would like to be like you," I confided, "whether I marry or not."

She put a hand on my arm. "I've had many challenges and met them. But I fear this one now will be my worst, having tea with the good Southern plantation mistresses of Andersonville," she said.

❧ · ☙

All the women from the surrounding plantations were waiting for us on the piazza of Pond Bluff. I felt myself go weak at the idea of meeting them.

Mr. Hampton was nowhere in sight, thank heaven. The women crowded around Miss Barton, exclaiming, praising, introducing themselves. None of them looked at me. But Miss Barton was not about to stand for that.

"This is my secretary," she said. "I believe you all know Eulinda?"

"Why, yes," came the surprised murmurings. Then there

was some talk about "My Sallie run off." Or, "How I do miss my Betsy. She could make the best chocolate cake."

They still saw me as a slave. My knees shook as we went into the dining room.

The same girl who was with Mistis the day she met us in town served. When everyone took their places around the dining room table I did not know what to do. I held back. Mistis came forward and greeted Miss Barton with a kiss. "Do come and sit." Then Mistis took her place at the head of the table where the good silver tea service lay waiting.

How many times I had polished those pieces. I knew every crevice, every delicate turn of the handles.

Miss Barton allowed herself to be led to a chair, but she did not sit down. Her hands gripped the back of it.

"And where does my secretary sit?" she asked.

Silence. And I thought, ain't that a thunderation! Her having such mettle. I waited, feeling the earth stand still.

"Why, of course, I forgot. Eulinda dear, bring that chair from the sideboard," Mistis directed. And then she whispered to Mrs. Hutchinson to her right, "I wouldn't do this for just any Negra girl, mind you. But Eulinda was once part of this household. And she is secretary to Miss Barton, after all."

I could not help noticing, as I brought the chair to the table, that the china she'd set out today was her second best.

The chatter was the usual at first. It was as if I'd never left. Whose daughter was expecting a baby, what the lastest news from Macon was, and how well the church choir had sung last Sunday.

Nobody spoke about the prison. They talked all around it. Somehow, I got through the tea. I think Miss Barton was very bored, but she smiled the whole time. Then, just as the ladies were walking her out to the piazza, Mistis called me back into the dining room.

"I know you have the ring," she said in a low voice. "And if you do not return it, I will send the provost marshal to arrest you."

"Mistis, I don't."

"Don't lie to me, you little thief. Neddy would never part with it. If you don't give it back, I shall have his grave dug up and searched. That ring is worth thousands of dollars and it does not belong to you."

I stood stunned, afraid to move. Around me the familiar objects seemed to shrink from my sight when I looked to them for comfort. No comfort there, only haunting accusation.

Dig up Neddy's grave? Was there no end to the evil in this woman? I could not permit that. Oh, what was I to do?

Then there was a footfall behind me. "Is something wrong?" It was Miss Barton.

"No," Mistis said. "We were just reminiscing a bit."

"Miss Barton, there is," I said. "Mistis says if I do not return a ring, she will send the provost marshal to arrest me, or dig up Neddy's grave."

"A ring? Why, Mrs. Kellogg, how could you?" Miss Barton said sweetly. "Eulinda has been my hardest worker and so good to everyone in trouble. I'm afraid you did not appreciate her when you had her around. You have no idea of the nature of the work we are all doing at the prison. How can you concern yourself with a ring? I tell you now, that if you do not leave this dear child in peace, I will exert every degree of power I have, and believe me, it is considerable, to have your true activities during the war brought to light."

I heard Mistis gasp.

"You see, I know you passed yourself off in Atlanta as a Secret Yankee in the war to make money. And a loyal Confederate here. Would you like that bandied about?"

Mistis shrank back. "I never," she said.

"I am here in Andersonville at the behest of our dear President Lincoln, who has since been killed. I am under the protection of Secretary of War Stanton," Miss Barton went on. "I thought you knew that my workers are also under their protection."

Then, before Mistis could reply, Miss Barton took my arm and we marched out. Only then was I aware of the quiet gasps of the ladies in the hallway. They had been listening.

I turned before going out the front door. Only then did I see the figure behind Mistis in the hall.

He must have heard the commotion and come out of his study. Mr. Hampton stood there. His hair was completely white now. He was disheveled, and he seemed stooped and old.

But he was having a good day. I could tell because he raised a hand in a sort of salute to me. He nodded his approval. I saw that before I went out the door.

CHAPTER NINETEEN

How I Give a Family a New Start and Finally Make Myself Come True

THAT NIGHT MR. WATTS TOOK A TURN FOR the worst and died. Miss Barton didn't come back to our tent until very late. But I was waiting up for her. She sat on her cot, her head in her hands. I decided this was the time.

"Miss Barton, I want to give you the ring," I said.

She looked up at me.

"Ring?" I could tell she was not here in this tent, but somewhere else, not here. Back home with her brothers, maybe. And I knew how, in bad times, it is always better to go back home inside your head to be with your brothers. Or sisters.

"The ring Mistis wanted. I want to give it to you. So

you can take Lily and her husband and babies back to Washington."

"Dear child," she looked at the ring I held out for her. "Are you sure?"

"More sure than I've been of anything," I told her. "It can give a whole family new life. And I'm sure Neddy would want that. And so would Zeke."

∿ · ∿

We stood together looking at the rows and rows of white headboards in the cemetery, Lily and I. There were now paved oval walks between the graves. All the fences were whitewashed. "Miss Barton said there will be Bermuda grass planted," I told Lily, "and this arch will have a big gilded eagle."

"I still wouldn't want to be buried here," she said.

∿ · ∿

Mr. Griffin called all the workers together on the sixteenth of August to tell us the work we had all contributed to was finished. "Tomorrow we will have a flag-raising," he said. "I am going to ask Miss Barton to raise the colors."

Everyone murmured approval. "Reporters will be here. We will have a supper for all the workers, then strike the tents tomorrow evening. Our work here is finished."

There were sounds of both joy and sorrow. We'd become like a family. The only family some of the Negro workers had, those who had lost family as slaves. Some of them did not want to leave. Mr. Griffin said he'd help find places for them all, if not as caretakers here, in other places in the area.

❧ • ☙

The next day, when Miss Barton was about to raise the colors over the cemetery, she turned to face the crowd. "I need a Negro worker to accompany me, because of the work you all did here," she said. "Come, Eulinda, for you have a brother buried on the hill. And another sold off in the time of slavery."

I felt a sense of peace. Tomorrow evening we'd get the train to Washington, Miss Barton and I, Dorence Atwater and his dead friend, and the Caters, including little Zeke. Even Otis.

I have made myself come true, I thought, as the flag went up the pole. Here, in this place, I have shed my old life and taken on a new one. And helped others to do so.

What is True and What Isn't in This Story and Some Plain Facts About the Real Characters

Andersonville Prison in Southwest Georgia was the most terrible prison, in either North or South, in the American Civil War.

Between February 1864 and May of 1865, 13,000 Union soldiers died at Andersonville. They died of starvation, disease, and lack of shelter and medical attention.

It was, in reality, a death camp—maybe the only real one to exist on American soil.

The story of those 13,000 souls is a massive one, and books have already done that story justice. My concern was with the people in the surrounding area and the simple but still unanswered question that applies not only here but to the areas in World War II Germany outside the death camps.

Didn't the people in the surrounding area know? I decided that since better people than I couldn't answer such a question, I'd create a family in the surrounding area, not white, but black.

I was most fascinated to find that black troops died in

Andersonville. And that Thomas Eston Hemings, a grandson of Thomas Jefferson, was one of them. There seemed to be such an irony in that. Especially since I had dealt with the subject of Jefferson's "black children" in my novel *Wolf by the Ears*.

All the incidents I mention in the book concerning the prison are true. Captain Henry Wirz was a Swiss immigrant, and spoke and acted exactly as I describe him. Indeed, he seemed to me like a forerunner of the concentration camp commanders in World War II. In the trial that followed the end of the war he was held responsible for the tragedy of Andersonville and executed in Washington, D.C., for his misdeeds on November 15, 1865.

There were three or four women prisoners in the stockade at the time. Mrs. Jamie Hunt and her husband were captured exactly as I have it. She did have her baby there and was taken in by neighbors. Women and sometimes young girls did climb to the parapets to view the prisoners like animals in a zoo. The prisoners did set up their own little town and even some forms of government inside the prison, and did sell all their valuables to get food from the suttlers, or peddlers, who came to the gates, or many more would have died.[1]

Dorence Atwater's story is true, also. Without his records the reburial and identification of the dead would not have been possible.

But before he and Clara Barton came to the prison, Mr. William Griffin arrived, an ex–Confederate officer who had heard how the wild boars and rats and dogs were disturbing the graves of the dead. Nobody knows his background. When I made a call to Andersonville National Historic Site (which now houses the national prisoner of war museum as well as honoring the Andersonville dead) I was told they were doing research but did not yet know the background of Mr. Griffin.

So he remains a mystery—just an ex–Confederate officer who decided to set the place to rights. As I have him doing, he employed local blacks to help him and paid them out of his own pocket. When General James Wilson, Union commander of the area, came along, he made Griffin superintendent of the place and paid him a salary, supplied him with food and, when Clara Barton came to Andersonville, supplied her with troops, black and white.

Again, the story of Clara Barton stands on its own and she can be read about in many books. She was, at the time, the most powerful woman in the country (although she could not vote). The wonders she had worked in the war, assembling help, supplies, medicine for the wounded, and setting up hospitals where there were none, were invaluable. And doubly impressive, considering the restrictions set upon women at the time.

And when she came to Andersonville she and Mr. Griffin worked together. With Dorence Atwater's death rolls they identified all the dead, reburied them, provided headstones, cleaned up the area, and landscaped it, and when she was not doing this she was helping local blacks who sought her out. She helped them to understand their newfound freedom, reading their rights to them, advising them, finding work for them, and creating order out of chaos.

Returning to Washington after Andersonville, Clara Barton did bring back Rosa and her husband, Jarret. Rosa became her housekeeper. I have her bringing back the Caters, Lily, Arnold, and their children. And, of course, Eulinda.

The Caters really existed and did come to seek her out at the prison. Eulinda, of course, and everyone else at Pond Bluff, are characters of my own making—although I did not have to stray far from history to create them.

Before she went to Andersonville, Clara Barton held a position in the U.S. Patent Office. When she returned, she found that it had been eliminated. Then she heard that Dorence Atwater was imprisoned for not giving up his register of death rolls. The government still did not want them published.

Atwater went to Auburn Prison in New York State, sentenced to eighteen months hard labor. Meanwhile requests were pouring in for Clara Barton to find missing soldiers. She approached the government to set up a bureau for her to operate out of. But the job went to someone else.

Clara decided to write a book about her experiences, but then found it would take $10,000 to publish it, while she had no backers. So she went into lecturing.

In December of 1865 Dorence Atwater was freed by a general order of President Andrew Johnson. Clara Barton worked behind the scenes to get his death register published, and finally on February 14, 1866, it appeared in Horace Greeley's *New York Tribune* in a special 74-page pamphlet. Atwater was called "one of the unquestioned heroes of the recent war." In recognition of her part in the work, Congress awarded Clara Barton $15,000 to continue tracking down missing soldiers. Clara hired a staff and reopened her Office of Correspondence with the Friends of Missing Men of the U.S. Army, which operated until 1868.

After this she criscrossed the country for two years on speaking engagements. She also defended the cause of the free slaves. Many veterans named their daughters after her. She went on to found the American Red Cross and at age seventy-seven served in hospitals in Cuba during the Spanish American War. She died in 1912 at the age of ninety.

She was, as I have in my book, fussed over and regarded as a celebrity in the town of Andersonville during her tenure at the prison. She was invited by local ladies to tea, although they never mentioned the subject of the prison while they entertained her.

There were Secret Yankees in Atlanta, remaining loyal to the Union in the midst of the Confederacy, and the activities of people like Mistis Jennie were a betrayal to them as well as to everyone around them.

Bibliography

Dyer, Thomas G. *Secret Yankees*. The Johns Hopkins
   University Press, Baltimore, Md., 1999.

Fox-Genovese, Elizabeth. *Within the Plantation Household.*
   The University of North Carolina Press, Chapel Hill, N.C., 1988.

Kantor, MacKinlay. *Andersonville*. New American Library,
   New York, N.Y., 1955.

Long, E. B., with Barbara Long. *The Civil War Day by Day.*
   Doubleday, Inc., New York, N.Y., 1971.

Lynn, Dr. John W. *800 Paces to Hell: Andersonville*, Sergeant Kirkland's
   Museum & Historical Society, Inc., Fredricksburg, Va., 1999.

McElroy, John. *This Was Andersonville.*
   McDowell, Obolensky, Inc., New York, N.Y., 1957.

Mellon, James, ed. *Bullwhip Days: The Slaves Remember.*
   Avon Books, New York, N.Y., 1988.

Oates, Stephen B. *A Woman of Valor: Clara Barton and the Civil War.*
   The Free Press, New York, N.Y., 1994.

Roberts, Edward F. *Andersonville Journey: The Civil War's Greatest Tragedy.*
   Burd Street Press, Shippensburg, Penn., 2000.